THE BITTER TRUTH

ALSO BY JANE GORMAN

A Blind Eye, Book 1 in the Adam Kaminski Mystery Series

A Thin Veil, Book 2 in the Adam Kaminski Mystery Series

All That Glitters, Book 3 in the Adam Kaminski Mystery Series

What She Fears, Book 4 in the Adam Kaminski Mystery Series

A Pale Reflection, Book 5 in the Adam Kaminski Mystery Series

THE BITTER TRUTH

JANE GORMAN

BLUE EAGLE PRESS

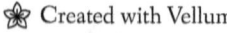 Created with Vellum

For Dorothy and Kerry

1

ELISE MARTIN FORCED herself to pick up her pace. Even after all these years, she still found herself slowing to admire the beauty of her adopted land. The shimmer of the mist rising from the valley, the complaints of Sandgrouse and high trills of Warblers from the copse of trees that bordered Thomas' fields, the air heavy with the scent of vines burning across the river — all buoyed her spirits and calmed her soul. But she had no time to dawdle today. She had plenty to keep her busy back at the café and the *chouquettes* tucked into the basket over her arm were gradually cooling. Andrew and Thomas would appreciate them even more if they were still warm from the oven.

She scanned the low mounds of the field ahead of her, sad reminders of the beauty that blossomed here only a few months previously, as her mind wandered over the tasks that lay ahead. Today was market day in *Fontaine-de-Vaucluse* so she knew she could count on fresh figs from Madame Dupont's stall. She still needed to have her lower oven repaired, hopefully Sebastien would be free to come today or tomorrow. And then there was the prep for the lunch and dinner customers. At least Andrew would be back by then and might be willing to help.

He'd left so early this morning, as he always did, with nothing more than a cup of coffee and piece of bread with jam, hoping for another day's work. At this time of year at Thomas' farm that just meant steaming out the weeds around the vines and lavender plants. Or perhaps some trimming remained or cleaning the presses that had only recently finished pressing out the last of the lavender oil that kept the farm successful.

Thomas had been hiring Andrew out periodically as a day laborer since they'd first arrived seventeen year ago. My God, she thought, has it really been that long? It was a precarious life for Andrew, not really knowing from day to day how much he'd earn, but they loved Thomas none-theless for taking a chance on them when they'd first arrived. When the rest of the village viewed them through distrustful eyes.

She turned right when she caught sight of the large Cypress that marked the boundary of the lavender field and the start of the vines that Thomas had only recently begun cultivating. Andrew would have been hard at work for the past two hours, so he and Thomas would be ready for a short break. The morning dew had long since dried as the sun sat midway up the horizon, shining bright in a perfect blue morning sky. She took a deep breath and allowed herself one more moment of appreciation.

The basket dangling from her right arm swayed as she walked, her other hand hanging loose by her side. Anyone who saw her, she imagined, would see only a local woman with nothing more on her mind than delivering her pastries while they were still warm. Anyone who knew her would think of her as bold, brave even, willing to pick up and move to a place where she didn't know anyone or speak the language. But some of her neighbors, the more insightful of the group — an image of the sharp-eyed Monsieur Bonnet came to mind immediately — might suspect that she carried something hidden in her dark eyes, in her faltering smile, in the fine lines around her eyes.

Her breath came a little heavier as she felt the incline of the field approaching the farmhouse, no doubt the result of the few extra pounds she carried around her hips, proof that she enjoyed eating French food as much as she enjoyed cooking it. She would have thought the long walks she'd taken every day for the past seventeen years would have been enough to keep her in better shape.

She was only a hundred yards or so from the farmhouse when she saw the tractor. It was the small one, the one Thomas used to spray heavy steam around the roots of the plants to kill any weeds that had the temerity to grow around his crop. How odd. It wasn't like Thomas to leave a piece of equipment out in the field like that. She knew from long, and sometimes painful, experience how fastidious he was with his equipment. One error on Andrew's part had been enough for him to learn his lesson. Thomas was kind to hire Andrew when no one else would, but he expected punctilious work in return. And a willingness to work for lower than standard wages as well, of course.

Elise switched directions and headed toward the tractor. Perhaps Andrew or Thomas were nearby and she just didn't see them. Though where they could possibly be hiding amongst these low, dormant plants wasn't clear. As she got closer, she felt her skin prickle in anticipation. Something was wrong. An unfamiliar scent floated on the slight breeze, even the birds fell silent as if watching her wary steps.

At ten feet away, she stopped. Her eyes scanned the field, took in the dark, quiet farmhouse, then shifted back to the tractor. Nothing moved. She took a step closer.

"Thomas?" The smallness of her voice surprised her and she coughed and tried again. "Thomas?" She called out this time, raising her voice to be heard as far as the farmhouse, in case he had run back inside for something. "Andrew?" She called again.

No answer.

She took a few more careful steps, then paused again. Was something leaning against the other side of the tractor? She walked to the far side, leaning forward to see. As her eyes connected with her brain, struggling to make sense of what she saw, the basket fell from her arm. *Choquettes* littered the ground around her. She opened her mouth but no sound came out, nothing to release the horror that enveloped her.

Thomas' body lay crumpled against the tractor, his legs splayed out in front of him, his arms by his sides, hands open, palms up. His upper body leaned awkwardly against the wheel well and his head fell back, exposing a mottled, white neck, his mouth hanging open. Blood had dried along the side of his head and left a sticky trail down around one ear and into the open collar of his jacket then pooled into a dip in the wheel well.

Elise stepped back and looked around frantically. Where was Andrew?

2

―――――――

"*Oui. Oui.*" Detective Adam Kaminski nodded vigorously, not caring how silly he looked. "*L'histoire.*" He offered what he hoped was a charming smile, even showing off his detested dimples.

The waitress returned his question with a look of skepticism. "*L'histoire de cette village?*"

Adam nodded and grinned again. "Yes, the history of this town."

This little town that nobody outside the area in the south of France known as the Vaucluse had ever heard of. A town of rosé wine and lavender, of locals chatting over their morning coffee in *tabacs* and bars just like this one. A town that got lost between the big tourist destinations of Aix-en-Provence and Avignon, not a town that drew many visitors looking for details of its mid-twentieth century history.

"*Un moment,*" the waitress said, turning toward the other end of the bar even as she said it. This *tabac* was not a large place. A small glass counter with a cash register offered displays of candies, newspapers and cigarettes. Opposite, two tall stools stood in front of a darkened wood bar. A few customers took advantage of the tables that sat in an open space beyond the bar.

Adam was beginning to think that the past few months of studying French hadn't paid off quite as much as he'd thought. He'd had more time than he'd wanted to prepare for this trip. It didn't matter how many vacation days he'd saved up, the new captain wasn't letting anyone take time off until the fiscal year rolled over. So he'd used the time to brush up on his high school French language and history and thought he was at least conversational by now. It had been a better use of his time than joining the other detectives in grumbling about rumors of inappropriate activity in the new captain's history. He preferred to resist the temptation of judging someone else's actions. Particularly given his own checkered past.

"Nico!"

Adam's thoughts were interrupted by the called greeting from a few patrons standing at the bar. A man in a black button-down shirt and jeans had slipped in quietly through a door behind the bar. He rolled his sleeves up to his elbows and wiped his hands on a towel as he passed by the patrons, avoiding eye contact with the customers who greeted him. Reaching the end of the bar, he wiped his hands one last time and tossed the towel over his shoulder.

He was a dark man, in appearance as well as clothes. His face was unlined but his hands were clearly used to work, clean but with the raw appearance of having been scrubbed often. Someone who'd worked all his life. If this was his bar, Adam thought, then he could be satisfied with the fruits of his labor. The man leaned forward, both hands on the bar, arms stiff, and nodded to the men near him. His eyes flitted around the room, belying the confidence that he otherwise exuded, and Adam noticed his hands shaking before he planted them on the bar.

"Nicolas." The waitress Adam had been talking with approached the man with an uplift of her chin, then spoke to him in French, far too fast for Adam to follow. They both glanced over at him as they spoke, so he didn't feel like he was stretching things to guess they were talking about him.

Finally, Nicolas stepped around the far end of the bar and approached Adam, his dark, lowered brow and frown giving him a look of nervous curiosity rather than anger. The waitress followed one step behind him.

"Nicolas, vous pouvez peut-être aider. Ceci est un Américain, il ne parle pas français."

Ouch. At least Adam understood that part. The waitress was explaining that Adam was an American who didn't speak French. He found it hard not to take that as an insult.

"Do you speak English?" Adam stood as he addressed Nicolas, putting out his hand.

Nicolas' grip was firm and cool. *"Oui.* A little bit," Nicolas said in a strong accent. He pulled the towel off his shoulder as he took a seat at Adam's table. Adam followed suit.

"This is a good thing," Nicolas said, eyeing Adam up and down. "To have an American visit our little town." He spoke pleasantly, but his dark eyes remained cautious. "I am pleased to see you. How can I help?"

"Thank you, that's wonderful." Adam answered with relief. "I'm looking for information about a school teacher who worked here during the war, one who may have been in touch with friends or colleagues in Poland. Specifically, I need to know-"

"Please, please." Nicolas held up a hand, cutting Adam off. "To speak more slowly, please."

"Right. Sorry." Adam thought through his question. What did he really want to know? "Is there someone in town who can talk to me about the history of this place? During the war?"

"The war?" Nicolas grinned. "*Vive la resistance*, you mean?" He laughed as he leaned back in his chair, as if releasing whatever tension he'd been holding. "We were quite the — how you say, the hot plate of resistance. You know this?"

"Not at all," Adam shook his head to make sure his meaning was clear. "No, I didn't know. And this is exactly the sort of thing I'm trying to learn."

Nicolas considered him carefully, and Adam could imagine what he saw. Despite his previous life as a history teacher and his careful efforts to be fair and kind, his years on the force had given him a hard look. He was a big man, tall with broad shoulders. That, combined with his rugged face showing his mixed Polish and Irish ancestry, led most to see him as a rough and tumble kind of guy.

Nicolas grunted. "Why do you want to know this?"

"It's personal," Adam answered. "I'm looking for some family history."

"Your ancestors are from France?" Nicolas asked without hiding the surprise.

What, did his round Irish nose and reddish hair not look French? "No, Poland."

"Ah ..." Nicolas nodded, his finger against his chin. "Perhaps one of our local teachers, then."

"Sure, that sounds promising."

Nicolas nodded firmly and stood. "*Moment.*"

Adam watched him walk back to the bar, sliding easily around the end. A group of teenagers waved to Nico as they passed outside and Nico nodded to them, gesturing toward the side door of the *tabac*. Adam shifted his attention to eavesdrop on the other patrons in the bar, hoping to prove to himself that his French wasn't as bad as the waitress claimed. It wasn't easy. The language these men spoke wasn't the perfectly enunciated, classic French of the lessons he'd been listening to.

A couple of middle-aged men huddled over small glasses of red liquor spoke loudly enough to be heard throughout the *tabac*. "Something strange, for sure," one said, taking a quick sip.

The other nodded. "I saw the same thing—" he started, but followed it with something Adam didn't understand.

"The police," the first man agreed. "And I didn't see Thomas anywhere."

A younger man who sat alone at a table in clothes that marked him out as an office worker rather than a farmer looked up at these words. Adam watched as he shifted his eyes from the newspaper in front of him to the two men at the table, then back to the newspaper.

A farmer at the bar joined into the conversation. "Chief Roche and Deputy Laconde were both there, at Thomas' farm," he said, turning to lean back against the bar and face the tables. "I saw them earlier."

The seated man nodded again. "And I'm sure I saw the doctor. Someone's hurt, no doubt."

The clean-looking young man in pressed trousers with his white button-down shirt open at the collar looked up, startled. "Who was hurt?" he asked the room in general. "Was Monsieur Lefebvre hurt?"

The men at the table shrugged and the man at the bar turned back to his espresso. "Who knows?"

A grizzled man, who appeared to be at least seventy, stood near Adam at the bar. His brown overalls and a plaid shirt marked him as a farmer, though his hands looked clean. Adam couldn't be sure if the overalls had originally been brown or had simply absorbed too many years of dirt and mud to show the difference. The man seemed to be listening to the conversations going on around him but offered nothing more than the occasional grunt.

The last grunt he directed at Adam. He'd been caught staring. He acknowledged the man, offering a pleasant, "Bonjour."

Instead of returning the greeting, or even ignoring it, the old man laughed out loud. "Bonjour, bonjour," he said loudly, echoing Adam's admittedly bad accent. "Comm-ent-allez-vous?" He spoke in an exaggeratedly slow manner, continuing to mock Adam's pronunciation, then laughed again, wiping his hand across his gray whiskers as he dribbled a bit with his laughter.

Adam felt his face grow hot, but tried to ignore the rudeness, turning his back to the old man. The farmer at the bar said a few words in harsh tones directed at the old man, so Adam chose to believe that this jerk's attitude was not shared by all the villagers.

Nicolas came back into the bar, this time patting the shoulders of patrons as he passed them. He clucked toward the old man as he walked back to Adam, waving a small piece of paper.

"For you. I write this down so you will remember."

"Thank you," Adam rose as he answered. "I really appreciate this."

"*De rien*, it is nothing, really." Nicolas glanced toward the old man, who was once again focused on his drink. "Ignore Enzo, he is, you know." Nicolas made a circling gesture near his head, one Adam easily recognized.

He offered his thanks again and looked at his watch.

Only eleven a.m. Nicolas had written that the school teacher wouldn't be finished with her classes until fifteen hundred, which Adam knew meant three p.m. So he had a few hours to kill. He'd come this far, he could wait a little longer to find the truth he needed to know.

————

ELISE LET HER STEPS SLOW. Why was she so nervous? She would find Andrew soon enough. Her brother was always in one of three places — at home, at the *tabac*, or at work on Thomas' farm. And she knew he wasn't at the farm. Chief Roche and his deputy had made sure of that, quickly scouring the area after their arrival and while waiting for the doctor.

She shuddered and shoved her hands down into her pockets. How would she tell him about this? They both loved Thomas like a father. This would crush him.

She looked around at the little town that had adopted them, welcomed them when they most needed it. No, they couldn't handle moving again. This was home, and nothing would chase her away this time. She continued on to find Andrew.

She nodded a greeting as she passed Madame Berger, one of her neighbors, two plastic bags hanging heavily from her reddened hands. Elise smelled the fresh tarragon dangling over the top of one bag before she saw it and let her mind wander to thoughts of what she would make for lunch today before remembering what she had just seen and swallowing the bile that rose in her throat. Madame Berger looked about to pause, a question plain in her eyes, but Elise hurried on, not ready yet to join in the gossip that must have already started, the moment the towns-

people realized something unusual was afoot in Thomas'
fields.

Thank goodness Chief Roche hadn't made her stay any
longer at the crime scene. It had taken over an hour as it
was, from the time she found Thomas, before they let her
leave. Chief Roche and Deputy Laconde had shown up
remarkably quickly, she'd been surprised by that. The local
police responding to what they believed could be a life on
the line. They didn't seem to want to take her word for it
that Thomas' life was no longer an issue. She'd never seen a
dead body before today, but there was no mistaking it.

They'd complimented her on how she'd handled herself
— not panicking, calling them immediately — then asked
what seemed like three hundred questions about where she
was going, where she was coming from, why she was cutting
through the field, how well she knew Thomas ... the questions became a blur in her mind.

Then they'd turned their attention back to Thomas.
Looking for clues, she assumed, some kind of sign that
would direct them to what, exactly, had happened. From
what she saw, it looked like a tragic accident. But then she
didn't have the mind of a police officer.

They'd left her standing in the field, waiting, as they
focused on the body. It was another fifteen minutes before
Chief Roche noticed her still standing there and let her
know she could leave. They knew where to find her when
they needed to. It was a small town.

Elise paused as she reached the thick stone walls of
Nicolas' *tabac*. The wide window that covered most of the
front of the shop was plastered with flyers and advertise-
ments for the lotto, local concerts and popular drinks. But
she could see enough of the interior to tell that Andrew
wasn't there. He must be at home.

Nicolas was talking with a stranger. A stranger in town was an unusual enough occurrence on its own, but Elise felt her pulse quicken. He looked around the *tabac* as he talked, making eye contact and smiling at the other patrons. It took only a glance for her to recognize the man as an American. A tourist, probably, though they didn't see that many tourists in their little town. A situation Nicolas was working hard to correct, she knew. Against the better judgement of a number of the older townspeople.

Had Nicolas succeeded in marketing their town to the throngs that visited the south of France every year? Or was this a solitary stranger, someone lost, perhaps, or someone who preferred to travel off the beaten path.

For a moment, just a moment, she considered going in. It would be wonderful to have a conversation with a fellow American. It had been so long since she'd done so. She and Andrew hadn't returned to the States after they fled, obviously. And she went out of her way to avoid anyone from their hometown of Baltimore, anyone who might know the story of their past.

But to speak English with a native speaker — American English at that. To share jokes that only other Americans would get, or reminisce about favorite foods or music. She felt her lips turning up into a smile and frowned.

That was not a good idea. This stranger could be a new friend, true, but he could just as easily be trouble.

She picked up her pace, hurrying home to find Andrew and break the news about Thomas, if he hadn't heard already.

3

AFTER AN HOUR or so of wandering the narrow streets of the village, Adam felt he had covered pretty much all of it. He meandered up and down cobblestone lanes lined with stone houses, some with geraniums flourishing in window boxes, others with brightly painted doors and shutters, all with curtains tightly closed. Walking by these dark, quiet houses, Adam thought the village could be deserted and he wouldn't be able to tell. Yet he knew that life went on around him.

At each of the two schools that served the young residents of the village, Adam heard the sounds of cheerful, vibrant life. Children called to each other from the playground behind one school. A teacher directed a group of older students toward a bus outside the other.

Other businesses in the village, however, did not share these outward signs of life. A gas station on the main street appeared to be open, but no attendants or customers were visible. A grocery store was clearly open for business — Adam could see a woman behind the register checking out a customer — but nevertheless the store seemed quieter, darker than Adam expected. Even on the wider streets that served as the main arteries for cars passing through the village he saw only a handful of vehicles. *Saint-Honoré* was clearly not yet on the tourist map.

He stopped for a moment at a gray monument that had been erected in a small park just off the main town square. Surrounded by grass, shrubs, two benches, and a cluster of red flowers, the monument stood like a miniature version of the Washington Monument. A plaque filled the lower half, lovingly cleaned of the dirt and grime that would have accumulated over the years. He couldn't make out all the names on the plaque, but he recognized the dates. The years of the Second World War. A memorial to those who had died.

He wondered if it was only those who had gone off to war who were memorialized here, or if the villagers had also recognized those who never had a chance to fight. The men, women and children who'd been carted off because of their religion, their ancestry. Designated for the camps of Drancy or Pithiviers or worse, Auschwitz.

Adam perched on one of the benches and thought about the quest that had brought him here. To France. To *Saint-Honoré*.

He'd been guided by a handful of letters he'd uncovered unexpectedly in Bermuda. Heartbroken at the breakup of his relationship and disgusted from learning that his great-grandfather may have collaborated with the Nazis, he'd needed a break. Thinking he was getting away from his problems on a cruise to the island, Adam had instead learned that the British had turned the former Hamilton Princess Hotel into one of their best counter-espionage resources during the war.

The apparent censorship station set up at what became known as Bermuda Station had served as a way-station for almost all of the transatlantic mail during the Second World War. Mail that included coded letters sent between his own great-grandfather and an unknown person from France. With the help of a librarian at Bermuda Station, Adam had not only discovered the letters but been able to trace their source to the very village in which the mysterious French person lived. The village of *Saint-Honoré*.

In fact, Adam stood, shaking himself out of his reveries, a librarian was exactly who he needed right now. He retrieved his car from behind his hotel and drove out to the large library in the nearby town of Cavaillon, driving past farmlands marked with low trees and vines. Unusual activity at one farm caught his attention — a cluster of cars, a group of people gathered near the main farmhouse. Perhaps this was the house he'd heard about this morning at the *tabac*. Where something bad had happened. Someone had been hurt.

He slowed as he passed, but didn't stop. This wasn't his concern. He continued his drive, passing nothing more exciting on the way than a cow that came a little too close to the roadside for his comfort.

The library at Cavaillon, referred to in French as the *Mediatheque*, was new and impressive. Tall, modern glass walls enclosed an open, airy space filled with all sorts of resources, from movies to music to art. And even books. Adam parked easily in the large lot behind the building, then followed a handful of other library patrons along the wide sidewalk to the front of the building.

Once inside, he stopped to get his bearing. A metal staircase divided the light-filled atrium, leading up to galleries on the second, third and fourth floor that themselves opened up onto the atrium as well. As welcoming as the hall felt, it wasn't immediately clear to him where he needed to go. He followed one sign that looked helpful but ended up in a room displaying photographs from local photographers. They were good, for sure, but not what he was looking for.

He must have looked as lost as he felt, because he felt a light tap on his arm and a soft voice whispered, "*Puis-je vous aider?*" May I help you?

"Yes, thank you," Adam whispered back. "I'm a little lost." He spoke in French, but unlike the waitress that morning, this librarian had no problem understanding his mangled pronunciation.

He managed to convey his interest in information about people in the area during the Second World War. She led him through a warren of rooms and levels, finding books, newspapers and microfiche that she explained would be of interest to him. Finally fully loaded with more than he could reasonably read, Adam followed her down one more flight of stairs, past a small tea shop to the main study room, where she set him up at a table with a computer and microfiche scanner.

She left him to his reading, offering to check in on him soon. Adam thank her profusely, then focused on what he'd been given. It didn't take him long to narrow his focus down to a number of newspaper accounts from the time when his great-grandfather would have been in Poland.

He wasn't really sure what he hoped to find in French articles from that time. Reference to Witold Kaminski, perhaps? He laughed softly to himself, knowing how unlikely that was. And after an hour of reading, he found that he was not wrong. No articles mentioned anyone by the name of Kaminski, no Polish visitors, no connections to Poland.

He struck gold, however, with a local history book

written by a man who lived right here, in *Saint-Honoré*. A retired teacher of history, the man had apparently spent his career studying the time of the war in France and its local impact. It wasn't a book Adam could easily peruse. Each page meant looking up ten new words, figuring out sentence forms he hadn't encountered before. But it was a start. He couldn't take the book with him, but now he knew where it was and knew he'd go back. To find the book. Perhaps to find the historian who wrote it.

4

_____

ELISE COULDN'T SHUT off the alarm bells going off in her mind. Andrew still hadn't surfaced. She'd checked everywhere she could think of. She even visited the garage where Sebastien worked, despite her distaste for the young man. Andrew, for some reason, had befriended Sebastien, so it was as good a place as any to look for him. But no luck there, either. Where else could he be?

She'd been back to her café, checking on progress for the lunch service as well as looking for Andrew. She kept reminding herself that she usually didn't see Andrew during the day, as they both went about their own business. But today wasn't a usual day.

Now she was back out on the streets and getting frantic. She caught herself looking in neighbors' windows as she passed and forced herself to stop. To think. As she stood there, a man turned a corner farther along the street, walking briskly in the opposite direction. She hadn't seen his face, but she'd know Andrew's gait anywhere.

"Andrew!" She yelled it out without thinking, then thought better of it and bit her lips. She walked as quickly as she could after his retreating form, scurrying along the sidewalk and hoping no one would be watching out their windows. A twitch of a curtain put that hope to rest. The villagers would be gossiping about her mad dash down the street later today, no doubt.

"Andrew." She called again, almost out of breath, as she finally got within a reasonable distance of her brother.

"Elise?" He turned, saw her leaning against a wall to catch her breath, and trotted back to her. "What's up?" He saw her expression and added, "What's wrong?"

"Andrew, do you know about Thomas?"

Andrew shook his head, a look of confusion on his face. "No, what?"

"Ah," Elise let out a breath. "Good." She felt her shoulders relax, then stood up straight again. "No, I mean, it's bad. Andrew, Thomas is dead."

The color drained from Andrew's face. He put out a hand to support himself against the wall, then glanced up and down the street. "What do you mean, he's dead?"

Elise raised a hand in a gesture of incredulity. "I don't know, Andrew. I don't know what happened. The police are there now. Trying to figure it out."

"There? Where?" Andrew's voice was sharp, but Elise couldn't tell if it was from grief or anger.

"At his farm. That's where I found him ..." her voice caught and she forced herself to breathe calmly.

"You? Oh, Sis." Andrew put an arm around her shoulder, drawing her close to him. She let his warmth comfort her for a moment, before pulling away.

"I found him in the field, Andrew. By his tractor. Where were you?"

"Me?" Andrew stepped back and frowned. "What do you mean, where was I?"

"You were supposed to be there, working ... I thought ..." Elise let her voice trail off as she saw the anger in Andrew's eyes.

"I always go to Thomas' first, yes. But you know as well as I do there's no guarantee of work. Just because I'm out for the day doesn't always mean I'm working for Thomas."

"No, of course, I know that." Elise kept her voice conciliatory, trying to calm her brother. "I just wondered—"

"Oh, I know what you were wondering." Andrew cut her off, stuffing his hands into his coat pocket and turning away from her. "The same thing you'll always wonder, whenever anything bad happens."

"Andrew." Elise put a hand on his arm but he shrugged it off. She looked away and saw that Madame Dubois had approached from a side street, but seemed to be slowing her steps to avoid interrupting their conversation.

"Madame Dubois," Elise acknowledged her neighbor with a greeting. "I apologize, we are blocking the path."

Madame Dubois nodded stiffly, then picked up her pace as she squeezed past the two Martins, pulling a wire cart behind her. Elise watched her go for a moment before turning back to Andrew.

"Andrew, I'm sorry, but I was worried about you. I really did think you were at Thomas'. And when I found him ... and you weren't there, well ... I was worried, that's all."

Andrew laughed. "What, you thought I was dead, too?"

"Well, why not?" Elise threw up her hands. "I had no idea what to think."

Andrew's expression didn't hide his disdain. "Oh yeah, you did. You knew exactly what to think. And it will never change. Never."

He turned as if to leave, then spun back toward her.

"You're right. I did go to Thomas' farm this morning, looking for work."

"And?" Elise whispered.

"And now I'm here," Andrew answered through gritted teeth. "That should be enough for you, Sis." The final word sounded like a hiss on his angry lips.

Elise watched him storm away, his back stiff, his hands deep in his pockets. She regretted angering him, she really did. She wanted to offer him unconditional support. She *did* support him unconditionally. But until they knew what had really happened to Thomas, Andrew couldn't afford to get angry. Not at her, and not at the police.

5

THE OUTDOOR TABLES at the café were empty at this time of day — too late for lunch, not quite time for an afternoon drink. Well, he was on vacation, so time didn't matter, did it, Adam told himself as he settled into a table tucked against the stone wall. From here, he could sit and watch the main square, watch the villagers passing through, stopping to chat, stepping into the stores that lined the square.

No waiter appeared to take his order. The café was clearly not ready for visitors at this odd time of the afternoon, but it didn't matter. Adam was happy to simply watch the village around him. He had to learn more about this village, these people. The connection with his great-grandfather was tenuous, he knew, but it was real. He was sure of it.

He let his mind work its way back through what he'd learned over the past few years: first, knowing from his childhood that his great-grandfather, Witold Kaminski, had left Poland during the war under mysterious circumstances. His cousin in Warsaw told him Witold abandoned the rest of the family when he'd left in disgrace. Adding to that, he'd later learned from the old German artist in Galway that Witold collaborated with the Nazis, which was how he escaped when he did. Who else had been able to escape Poland in 1940, wife and son in tow? But, finally, the letters from Bermuda Station. Letters that suggested not collaboration, but resistance. Resistance and fear.

Adam pulled out his phone while he waited, scrolling through the letters he'd scanned and emailed to himself. Letters that offered a glimmer of hope that his great-grandfather hadn't been the monster everyone thought.

"Made it safe to France," he wrote into his phone. "Glad you're not here." He grinned as he sent the message to Pete, his partner on the force back in Philadelphia. "How're things at home?" He sent a second text.

As he waited for Pete's response, he thought about what he knew, the history of this country, this town, his own family. Small details of the village around him came into focus. Pockmarks in the wall of a building might have been bullet holes. An elderly woman making her slow, painful way along the far stretch of the square was probably a survivor of the war itself. What stories could this town tell? What had the old church witnessed throughout those dark years?

A ding from his phone let him know Pete was up and about. Not surprising. He was probably already at his desk, working away on the endless reports, spreadsheets and authorizations that were a drag on police work in Adam's mind but that Pete was always willing to tackle.

"Same as always," came the texted response. "Captain Hillyard's on a rampage. Again. You'll be working overtime when you get back."

He replied with an appropriate emoji, then added. "Glad to know you've got things covered." The words were tongue-in-cheek. Pete always had them covered. The one person Adam knew he could always count on. Always trust. Even with his life.

"Take care, partner. And good luck." Pete texted.

Adam dropped his phone onto the table, clasping his hands together on his lap, peering at the town around him and the people as they passed.

"Hey! *Qu'est ce que tu regardes?*" What are you looking at? The words came out as a sneer from one of the young men crossing the square toward the café and Adam knew enough French to recognize the insult in the use of the informal "you."

The trio of men — and as they got closer, Adam realized they ranged in age— wore stained overalls, their hands blackened from their work. Which, based on the smell of oil as they approached, Adam assumed was in a garage somewhere.

"Hm?" The first young man said again, lifting his chin.

Adam raised both hands in a friendly gesture. "*Pardon,* I am sorry." He was pretty sure this young buck wouldn't appreciate hearing Adam's internal thoughts on the war, on the repercussions of that era of cruelty that were still being felt today.

A middle aged man approached Adam's table just as the young men did. "Ignore them," he smiled and spoke slowly and clearly. "They are just making trouble."

The angry young man grinned, his eyes narrowing. "Perhaps I like trouble, eh?" He turned and laughed at his colleagues who seemed more embarrassed than amused by the encounter.

"Come on, Sebastien, leave it," the older man in the group commanded.

Sebastien gave Adam one more glare then turned to follow his friends up a side street.

"What the hell was that about?" Adam asked, turning to face the man next to him. "What the fuck, I was just sitting here?" He took a breath. "Sorry, I apologize for my language."

The man laughed. "*De rien, monsieur*. We are not saints around here. No," he waved a hand vaguely in the air, "do not worry about Sebastien and his colleagues. They are just not used to seeing strangers in town."

Adam let out another breath, feeling his heart rate return to normal. "I guess not. Is that how they treat everyone who passes through? What are they afraid is going to happen?"

The man shrugged, lifting both shoulders with his hands open wide. "Who is everyone, *monsieur*? We do not get many visitors to this town. For now, at least."

Adam gave him a curious look, encouraging him to go on.

"Well," he leaned forward conspiratorially. "Nico is trying to change that, no?"

"No?" Adam repeated.

"*Oui*," the man nodded with satisfaction as if he'd just won some type of argument. "He will try to get more people to visit our town." He shrugged again. "But we shall see. Not everyone is ready, I think, for this."

Adam shook his head as he stood, thanking the man for his timely intervention. What kind of crazy town had he come to? He knew he needed help, but it was becoming apparent that the locals wouldn't be jumping up to help him any time soon. Not the most welcoming bunch.

He knew enough about himself to know that he was letting his temper get away from him. Again. He took a couple more deep breaths. It was time to visit the school-teacher Nico had recommended. Though if this morning was anything to go by, he should keep his expectations low. She'd probably be as unfriendly as the rest of this cursed town.

6

————

THE SCHOOL'S brownish-red stones matched those of the buildings on either side. All the buildings that lined the narrow street, in fact. It was as if the town has been carved out of the rock of the mountain that rose behind it, offering a romantic view of mist covered slopes.

Adam pulled on the rust-red door and it opened with a sharp creak. He grimaced and glanced around, but he hadn't drawn any attention. Which was unfortunate, since he wasn't entirely sure where he was going. He checked the slip of paper Nicolas had given him, then looked up and down the hall that ran to his left and right.

He turned left.

The building was utilitarian. Fluorescent lights lined the ceiling and square, glass-fronted cases broke up the monotony of the brick wall in equally measured spaces. The cases held notices of some sort, though Adam couldn't decipher them all.

He paused to look at a series of photographs in one of the cases, groups of students clustered around their teachers, he assumed. Class photographs, perhaps. Or maybe teams, he couldn't be sure. He saw young, smiling faces with the occasional saturnine student thrown in here or there. It brought back fond memories.

He missed being a teacher, he knew that. He'd enjoyed his time working with young people in Philadelphia, sharing his interest in history, in the stories about people's lives long ago. And some of his students even seemed to share his interest. Well, some of them, certainly not all.

He didn't regret leaving, though. Not after the tragedy. After one of his students was killed in a drive-by shooting while doing nothing more than sitting on the front stoop of his house in Northwest Philadelphia, Adam realized he'd make more of a difference in law enforcement than teaching. At least now, as a cop, he was keeping them safe. Them and all the other kids in the city who deserved a chance to learn, to grow up, to live. His face hardened and he focused on why he was here. To find the truth, no matter how unhelpful the villagers turned out to be.

He kept walking down the hall, heading toward a door ahead on the right with a sign hanging over it. That looked promising.

As he expected, the door led him into a small office. A woman in metal-framed glasses sat behind a tall counter tapping away at her computer.

"*Bonjour madame,*" he interrupted her work.

"*Bonjour.*" She looked up, her expression making it clear that she didn't appreciate the introduction.

"Yes, hi," Adam continued in French. "I'm looking for Margot Roche, a teacher here. Madame Roche?"

"You are looking for Madame Roche? Why? Who are you?" The surprise in her voice was tinged with suspicion.

Adam dug out the note from Nicolas. "Here," as he

spoke he struggled, as always, with the pronunciation. "I was told to find Madame Roche by Nicolas. At the *tabac*."

"*Oui*," the woman nodded, glancing at the note. "One moment." She flicked one hand toward Adam as if dismissing him and picked up her phone. As she dialed, she looked at him expectantly. He took a step back, assuming she was asking for privacy. Though he could still hear everything she said.

Her call to Nico was brief. Based on what he could understand of her end of the conversation, Adam figured he was telling her everything he knew about Adam. Which wasn't much.

She hung up and glanced at the clock hanging on the wall behind her, then back to Adam. "She is still teaching her class," she said in slow English. "*Alors*, you can wait." She waved a hand toward a bench next to the door.

Adam glanced toward the bench, but instead of sitting he walked over to a series of diplomas hanging on one wall. He saw various levels of degrees, some from schools he'd never heard of, others from internationally prestigious universities. Impressive, actually. He was searching for Margot Roche's name when a bell rang, followed immediately by children's shouts and calls. More memories attacked him, though the teenagers he'd taught had called out in lower, angrier voices.

He returned to the woman at the front counter. When she didn't look up, he coughed.

"Ah, yes," she nodded and stood. "Follow me."

He did, side-stepping children as they hurtled down the corridor towards them, eager to escape their imprisonment in the school. Adam followed the woman through the halls until she stopped in front of an open door. She tapped on the frame then entered. Adam stopped just inside the doorway, unsure if he'd been invited in or not.

A teacher stood behind an old, battered wood desk at the front of the classroom. The age of the desk clearly did not reflect the quality of the teaching equipment, however, as a white board glowed behind her on the wall.

She looked up as they entered, running one hand through her short hair as she did so, leaving thick red hairs standing on end. Adam wondered if her red hair hinted at some Irish or Scottish ancestry.

The receptionist spoke to the teacher in rapid fire French that Adam couldn't understand. Margot Roche asked only one question, then they both looked at Adam, the receptionist with suspicion, the teacher with curiosity.

He put his hand out as he approached her. "Good afternoon, Ms. Roche? I'm Adam Kaminski."

"American," she said with surprise, as if she hadn't believed the receptionist when she told her. "Yes, I am Margot Roche. Can I help you?"

"I hope so," Adam said, watching as the receptionist left the room. He looked back at Margot. "Do you have a few minutes to talk?"

She looked down at the slim golden band on her wrist, frowned and wagged her head back and forth in indecision. "Perhaps just a moment. Please, have a seat."

Adam sat in the front row of the students' chairs and she perched on the desk in front of him. A beautiful woman, Margot seemed to go out of her way to hide her beauty. From the short, boy-cut hair to the long, simple gray skirt she wore with flat shoes and a flowered sweater. Then again, she was teaching young boys. Perhaps she was wise to dress down.

"I'm trying to learn something about a person who lived

here, in this town, during the war." Adam explained. "It's for some research I'm doing about my family history."

"Your family?" she asked. "Is your family from France?"

"No," Adam shook his head. "Poland. But I have reason to believe my great-grandfather either was here, or worked closely with someone who lived here." He shrugged and made a face, "To be honest, I'm not entirely sure and I don't have a lot of information. That's why I'm here."

Margot seemed to consider what he'd said, chewing on the cap of the pen in her right hand. "I see," she finally said. "So perhaps you are interested in Vichy France, then?"

"Perhaps, I'm not sure."

"You are familiar with the Vichy regime?" she asked.

"Of course," Adam didn't appreciate the implication. Of course she would think an American wouldn't know about the French government that had collaborated with the Nazis when France had been occupied during the war. He also knew that most French today doubted the wisdom of that collaboration. Had their efforts helped to save France? Or curse her?

Margot nodded. "This was a bad time in France, you know? Many people do not like talking about it. Are you sure you want to dig this up?"

"I'm not trying to dig up old ghosts." Adam heard the defensiveness in his voice and took a breath, trying to calm down. He was here asking for help, after all. "I'm trying to put one away, to let it rest in peace. We have a story in my family, passed down through the generations. About my great-grandfather, you see?"

Margot nodded, the confusion evident in her eyes.

Adam continued, "I recently found evidence that the story may not be true. I need to find the truth." He stopped, not sure how to explain this need. His sister Julia certainly hadn't understood when he'd explained it to her. It was her family, too. He couldn't understand why she didn't care as deeply as he did. Hopefully, she would at least appreciate it when he found the truth.

"The history is important to me," he finished, knowing it was a lame explanation.

Margot took a breath. "It is interesting, I am sure, to learn about your family. But you must not disturb those of this village who have put the past behind them. Who have moved on."

"No, of course not." Adam stood up. "I can see that this was a mistake, I'm sorry to have bothered you."

"No." Margot stood as well, putting a hand up to stop Adam. She smiled, "Please, sit, I did not mean I cannot help. I simply—" Her phone rang, cutting her off. She dug through the oversized purse on her desk and pulled out her phone. Her conversation was brief.

When she turned back to Adam, her demeanor had changed, her relaxed smile replaced with furrowed brows and worried eyes.

"I'm sorry, it's just ... that was my husband, Chief Roche."

"Chief?" Adam asked.

"He is the Chief of Police for *Saint-Honoré*," she waved away the explanation even as she offered it. "There has been an accident. A tragedy. Someone is dead."

Adam caught his breath. "A murder?"

She looked at him as if forgetting who he was. "A murder? Perhaps, I don't know. He just let me know he would be late getting home."

She shook her head and softened her expression. "I apologize, that caught me by surprise. The job of the Chief of Police in a town like this does not often involve death. We will be seeing the *gendarmes*. Julian will not want to ..." her expression faltered, then she shook her head. *"Monsieur*, let me think about your request. I am sure there are people here in the village who can help you. We must be careful, that is all, so as not to upset anyone."

Adam stood. "Thank you. I appreciate any help you can offer me, I really do. Can we meet again, perhaps tomorrow?"

"Of course." She shook his hand once more. "Then we shall see what you can learn about our little town and the people in it."

7

Elise kept her attention focused, as always when starting the dinner service, on the kitchen. Helene was waiting tables that evening, so Elise knew she didn't have to worry about the front room. She kept an eye on the *chouquettes* in the convection oven, or more accurately a nose, since she had developed the skill of knowing exactly when to pull them out based on the caramel scent of the buttered almonds. She had earned her reputation with these signature pastries.

As she waited, she watched with satisfaction as Henri manned the grill, turning out succulent legs of duck and spicy sausages. This would be a lot easier if her lower oven was working. She lent a hand to chop a few more carrots and green beans then lay down her knife as she sensed the pastries were ready to come out.

When the pastries were safely cooling on the rack, she wiped her hands down her apron and pushed out through the swinging door into the main dining room, prepared to greet the regular customers. Her steps faltered when she saw the American stranger.

He sat at a small table tucked against the wall just beyond the front window. He was eating alone, a glass of red wine on the table in front of him, the bottle left to breathe on the sideboard to his right. She recognized the label. He'd made a good choice in wine, or Helene had advised him well.

There was no good excuse – or reason, really – to avoid him now.

"*Bonsoir, monsieur.* Welcome to my café."

The man had offered a bland smile as she started in French, but he sat up in surprise when she switched to English.

"You're American," he said.

"I am," she replied. "Elise Martin. I run this café. May I join you?"

The man stood and gestured to the other chair. "Of course. Please do."

Elise raise a finger toward Helene, who brought a second glass. He poured her some wine and Elise raised her glass in a toast. "*Santé.*"

"*Santé.*" The man took a sip with her. "I'm sorry, I should have introduced myself. Adam Kaminski. From Philadelphia. Tell me, how did a woman from the States end up running a café in *Saint-Honoré*?"

Elise shrugged. "Life can take some interesting turns, can't it? Are you here visiting someone?"

"You could say that." Adam laughed and dimples appeared on either side of his smile, making his rugged face look boyish and charming. "I'm hoping to learn something about someone who lived here a few years back. During the war."

"The Second World War? Are you a historian then?"

"I am, actually. Not professionally, at least not anymore.

And I guess I've lost whatever skills I used to have because I don't seem to be getting very far, very fast in this town."

Elise laughed. "No one moves fast in *Saint-Honoré*, Mr. Kaminski."

Helene interrupted their conversation with a sizzling plate of steak with fries, the pungent red wine and mushroom sauce reminding Elise that her own lunch, the main meal of the day for her, had been several hours earlier.

Adam paused with his fork and knife in his hands.

"Please, eat. Don't mind me," Elise said. "Unless you prefer to eat alone?"

"Not at all, I appreciate the company."

Elise watched as Adam cut a slice of steak, catching a few mushrooms on it before eating it. She took a sip of wine to give him time to eat, admiring the strength she saw in his hands, his arms, his shoulders.

"Now tell me, who is it that you want to learn about?"

"A man who was a schoolteacher here. A man who may have had contact with another teacher in Poland."

"During the war? You're talking about the resistance then."

"Maybe I am," Adam shrugged before chewing another piece of steak. "A teacher here, Margot Roche ..." He paused to take a drink and Elise nodded her familiarity with Madame Roche. "She said she might be able to help me."

Elise nodded, thinking. "She is a history teacher. That sounds like a good start. There are others in our town familiar with the time as well."

"Our? How long have you lived in this town, Elise?"

Long enough for her to be a little surprised by his familiarity. But she knew it was the American way. "Long enough," she answered. "We came when I was in my twenties."

"We?"

"My brother and myself. Andrew."

"And is Andrew still here as well?"

"He is."

Adam must have picked up on the reluctance in her voice, born of years being afraid to share too much about their past and nurtured by the natural French reticence. He switched topics, launching instead into a detailed story about his own planning for his visit to France.

"I practically had to beg for the time off, which drives me crazy because I've got more than enough leave saved up. Plus some extra money since my last vacation ended up being comped." He glanced over at her. "Sorry, I'm babbling a bit. Just city politics back at home."

"You work for the city?" she asked.

"Not exactly. I'm a cop. A detective with the Philadelphia Police Department." He paused. "Are you ok?"

Elise thought she'd hidden her shock behind her wine glass. "Of course, of course." She shook her head. "I apologize, I really should get back to work."

She put her hand on the table, ready to stand, but a touch on her arm cause her to sit back. "Deputy Laconde."

The young police officer looked exhausted, his uniform dirty and wrinkled, his eyes red and his cheeks gray. "Mademoiselle Martin. We are looking for Andrew. Do you know where he is?"

"Andrew?" Her voice wavered, and she coughed. "My apologies," she said to Adam in English. "This officer is looking for my brother."

He smiled. "I understand, you speak very clearly."

She turned back to Laconde. "I'm sorry, I don't know where he is right now. He's not here. Is it urgent?"

"We must speak to him, Mademoiselle. About Thomas Lefebvre."

Elise glanced at Adam, but he nodded. "I heard there'd been a tragic accident."

The officer raised an eyebrow but did not respond.

"I will try to find him. I can tell him to find you. At the police station?" Elise felt her voice rising and took a breath to calm herself.

Laconde nodded grimly. "*Merci, mademoiselle.* If he can come in the morning. We can speak with him then."

"I hope that means you're going home to get some rest?"

He nodded and offered another grim smile to both of them. "Perhaps. *Bon soir.*"

Why would they want to talk to Andrew again? That made no sense. Everyone knew how much she and Andrew loved Thomas. He'd hired Andrew to work in his lavender fields, even without work authorization. He'd made them feel welcome. Elise and Andrew owed him so much.

Elise realized she'd shredded the paper napkin in her hands. And that the Philadelphia cop was watching her closely.

"I don't know where Andrew is. I'll have to find him," she said, standing.

Adam stood as well. "I'm so sorry. I know how difficult an investigation can be. Even for innocent bystanders. Especially for innocent bystanders. If there's anything I can do to help, please ask."

"Thank you, you're very kind. I really don't know why I'm acting like this."

"It's completely understandable. No one wants to be involved in an investigation, particularly about death."

8

"BONJOUR MONSIEUR KAMINSKI. I hope our meeting isn't too early for you?"

Adam started when he heard Margot's voice, drawn out of the reverie the town square had inspired in him.

"Not at all. I enjoy getting up early," Adam answered as he rose to greet her, then helped her into a chair at the small round café table. Their seats both faced out onto the square, an opportunity to observe the townspeople going about their daily tasks.

Adam wasn't just being polite. He really did enjoy getting up early. He'd risen before the sun this morning, making his way slowly from his hotel to the café where he and Margot had arranged to meet. He found himself torn between a desire to explore each narrow alley he passed and the stronger desire for a good cup of coffee. Not surprisingly, the coffee won out.

He'd arrived at the café just as they were setting out the chairs on the wide sidewalk. He watched as a waiter brushed the last one down, then gestured to request a seat.

The waiter simply waved a hand over the entire area and shrugged. Sit anywhere, he supposed.

While he sat, he watched. A few children passed, bags slung over their shoulders, getting in to school early perhaps. Teenagers as well, on their way to the local *lycée* or high school most likely. The adults were harder to place. Shop-keepers, perhaps, some teachers, some farmers. He tried to imagine the daily life of each person he saw, what kind of routine they followed in a small town like this. He tensed when he saw the young man in oil-stained denim overalls. He felt his adrenalin rising, but the young man hadn't noticed him. Or didn't care to start a fight today. Unlike yesterday. He turned his attention back to the unknown pedestrians.

He'd already downed one espresso before Margot inter-rupted the life stories developing in his head.

She flagged down a waiter and ordered a coffee for herself. Adam took the opportunity to get another for himself and a brioche with jam.

"I have been thinking more about your questions, Monsieur Kaminski, and I am convinced Monsieur Bonnet is the best person for you to speak with." Margot explained as she took one sip of her coffee. "He is a historian here in town. I can speak to you, of course," she added quickly when Adam started to speak. "Yes, I am happy to. But this man, Monsieur Bonnet, he knows far more than I about this time period. He is our expert, you see." She smiled as she spoke, her hazel eyes lighting up, and Adam felt his spirits lift.

Finally, something good. "Bonnet? I recognize the name. I saw a book by him in the library yesterday. I was hoping to find him."

"You have read his book?" Margot didn't hide the

surprise in her voice, and Adam felt that familiar thud of disappointment in his gut. He resented being underestimated like this.

"As best I could, yes. Look, thank you so much for this suggestion. How should I find him? Will you introduce us?"

Margot shrugged. "I suppose I could, but then you would need to wait until I had some time available. It would be easier for you, I think, to go on your own."

He watched as she took a second sip of her coffee and placed the empty cup back on the table. These were quick drinks, not like lingering over a latte at an American coffee shop. He pulled another piece of brioche apart and covered it in jam before eating it.

"I understand you are a history teacher as well," he said.

Margot nodded. "Yes, but I teach very basic history of France. I don't have the detailed knowledge of our own town that Monsieur Bonnet has." She paused, frowning. "But I should warn you about him."

"How so?" Adam asked lightly, not sure what to expect.

"He takes his history very ... em, very seriously." She finally settled on a word. "This is a subject he is passionate about."

"That's great. I admire that."

"Yes, yes. But you must understand. It is personal for him."

Adam held up his hands in agreement. "I get that. I'm asking these questions because I want to find the truth about my great-grandfather — who he really was, what he did, why he left Poland. It's personal for me, too."

"Good, that is good." Margot nodded slowly. "Monsieur Bonnet does not like the Vichy regime."

"Was he alive then?"

"No, no," Margot laughed lightly. "But his family was

here, in the town. They were part of the resistance, and they suffered for their efforts. He remembers that as if it were yesterday."

Adam thought about how easy it was to pass grudges on from one generation to the next, to hold the son responsible for the sins of the father. "Hopefully that doesn't make it harder for him to live here."

Margot shrugged again and frowned. "In some ways, I believe it does. There are other families who were part of the official government. Who supported the Vichy. Families like the Dubois, the Lefebvre." She frowned again, and blinked her eyes. "To Monsieur Bonnet, it is as if they were the criminals themselves. No," she shook her head. "There are some villagers who will not like that you are digging into the past."

Adam waited a moment, to give himself time to consider what she'd told him and to give her time to walk her mind away from thoughts that clearly saddened her.

"Tell me about this town," he finally said. "Today, I mean, not just historically. What's it like to live here?"

Margot's lips formed into a soft smile as she looked over the square. "It is a beautiful place to live, Monsieur. There could be nowhere better. We have our farms, our vineyards, our food." She shrugged and looked back at him. "Is that what you mean?"

Adam nodded. "It does seem peaceful."

"Ah, it is." Margot took a breath. "Even being married to the chief of police, it is peaceful." She paused. "Usually."

"You're thinking about the death. Yesterday."

Margot nodded. "This is a small town, a wonderful town filled with friends. I worry that Julien will struggle if this is not an accident. If there must be an investigation into the death of Thomas Lefebvre."

"Lefebvre? The name you just mentioned a moment ago, one of the families who collaborated?"

"*Oui*. But Thomas was a good man." She cast her eyes down to the table and her empty cup. "He was not responsible for the past any more than I am. And now he is dead."

"Will your husband lead the investigation then?"

"No, no." Margot lowered her brow as she shook her head. "There is not yet a true investigation. They must wait for the cause of death. Perhaps it was a tragic accident, you see."

"Ah." Adam did not see, but bit his tongue.

"If there is to be an investigation, Julien will call in the *gendarmes*. He will have no choice ..." her voice faltered and she looked away, over Adam's shoulders.

"And is that a problem?" he probed. It wasn't his business, he knew, he just couldn't resist.

She looked back at him as if bringing herself back to the present. "Of course not. Now, I must go. Good luck to you, Monsieur Kaminski."

And good luck to your husband, Adam thought but he didn't say it out loud. He didn't understand how the French police system worked, but from what Margot had said, it seemed like Chief Roche would need all the luck he could get.

9

"Mademoiselle Martin," Chief Roche sounded like he was trying to sound patient. "I am aware you have concerns for your brother. But we must speak with him alone. You understand." He dipped his head and waved his hand toward the door of the office.

"But I should be present, shouldn't I?" she asked. "I am his legal guardian."

Even Andrew rolled his eyes at that. "You *were* my legal guardian, sis," he said, switching to English. "That was a lot of years ago."

Why was Andrew being so calm about this? Elise played with the fringes of her scarf, accidentally pulling it tighter around her neck. She stuck a finger in-between her scarf and her skin to loosen it.

"*Monsieur Roche...* Julien." Elise reverted to French. "You know us. You know we weren't involved in this. We loved Thomas. He was like a father to us." She looked to Andrew for confirmation, but he just looked at his feet.

They were standing in the small office that Julien Roche claimed as his own, an even smaller antechamber with only a desk and a hard wooden bench waiting for her just beyond the office door. The offices were tacked onto the back on the town's *Mairie,* or town hall, an addition built only ten years earlier when the town had agreed to the mayor's request to budget for its own police force.

Though Julien claimed the title of Chief of Police, it was not as grand a position as the title might imply. In fact, Julien was the only full-time police officer on staff. He also had an assistant, Deputy Laconde, but Laconde worked part-time at a local grocery as well as with Chief Roche. Perhaps that explained Julien's remarkable success rate at catching what few criminals there were in the little town of *Saint-Honoré.* Secrets were spilled like salt as neighbors gossiped at the store, and part-time Officer Laconde was there to hear them. But an investigation of this magnitude was surely beyond his jurisdiction.

She'd brought Andrew in as soon as she knew Julien would be there. Immediately. That was the act of an innocent person, wasn't it? Julien must recognize that they had nothing to hide. At least, not anymore.

"Elise," Julien's switch to first names comforted her, though she suspected it made Julien less comfortable. "I know that you are worried because of the past."

She nodded, chewing her lip.

"I am aware that your moving to France was not ..." Julien frowned as he struggled for words. "Not entirely planned, shall we say."

Elise nodded again. Julien had known about their flight to France for years now. Knew that they had arrived in France as simple tourists, with no visas, and decided to stay. Knew that they had both found work even without permits, joining the underground labor market that officials like Julien swore to stop.

"And you also know that we fixed that error. Years ago. We both have residency permits now. We both have work permits."

"And Thomas hired Andrew before that happened." Julien's voice was stern.

Elise let out a breath when Andrew finally spoke up. "He didn't have to do that, he was trying to help us. That's all. He wasn't hurting anyone."

"Whether or not illegal immigration hurts anyone is not the matter at hand, Monsieur Martin." Elise flinched as Julien reverted to his normal, formal form of address. "You were involved in a criminal activity with the victim. Therefore we must question you about his death." He looked directly at Elise. "Alone."

"But it makes no sense, Julien. Think about it. Why would Andrew hurt Thomas?" She asked again. "We're here, we've told you we had nothing to do with this. What other questions could you have?"

Julien's grin at this was real, he almost laughed. "Elise, we have other questions." His face returned to its stern expression. "You must know, I am aware of Andrew's history."

Elise felt her face blanch, felt weak in the knees. Andrew didn't move, didn't flinch.

"You know?" her voice came out as a squeak.

Julien nodded. "I looked into all unusual circumstances when I took on this position. You and your brother, well, you are unusual."

Elise felt her anger flare. "How so? Americans can move to France, can't they? I'm sure it happens all the time."

"Yes, of course," Julien spoke calmly. "But nevertheless, I checked. I am aware of your past."

Elise felt her lips tremble. How could Andrew be taking

this so calmly? To have been suspected of murder once had been tragic. Life changing. They'd fled their home, their friends, their lives, to get away from it. And now it had found them. In the one place she'd thought they'd be safe.

"Andrew, we have to leave. We have to find a lawyer. Or something, I don't know." She realized she was muttering, looking around the small office as if she could find something — anything — that would get them out of this.

"Sis," Andrew's voice was calm. "It's okay. I didn't kill Thomas. You know that." He glanced at Julien. "Chief Roche knows that. This isn't even a murder investigation. But he needs to talk to me."

Andrew's rational attitude only scared her more. Did he know something she didn't? If he did, that could only be bad. But how could he be involved in something like this? Not after what they went through in Baltimore. Not after all they'd given up to restart their lives.

"Elise, this is necessary." Julien took one step toward the door and pulled it open even wider, gesturing again with his other hand.

She pulled on her scarf again as she looked back and forth between the two men, one firm and determined, the other oddly calm and resigned. This wasn't good.

She passed through the door and perched on the hard wooden bench in the antechamber as the door to Julien's office closed behind her with a purposeful click.

10

THE ANTEROOM in which Elise waited was more hallway than room. Laconde's small desk sat at one end, a few feet beyond the door to Julien's office to her left. The glass-paned front door stood no more than fifteen feet to her right. Elise shifted her weight on the hard bench but couldn't relax. What was Julien asking Andrew? More importantly, what was Andrew telling him?

Laconde had joined Julien for Andrew's interrogation (though they insisted on calling it an interview), so she sat alone with nothing to spare her mind from its worst thoughts. Images of Andrew thrown into a French jail, crowded with fears of what she would do if she lost him.

She jumped when the front door swung open, bringing the sounds of the street outside in with the intruder. How incongruous, she thought: this modern glass door holding out sounds of cars and passing trucks while her thoughts were of ancient, dank French prisons, like the Bastille or Clairvaux. While the room in which she waited was fully equipped as a modern office, she could picture the worn stone exterior, a building that had housed the town's mayor for hundreds of years.

"Elise?" Camille Lambert slid next to her on the bench, lifting a hand to fiddle with a lock of pale hair that draped over her shoulders. "I didn't expect to see you here."

Elise shared a nervous smile with Camille. "No. I didn't expect to be here."

"I see." Camille nodded, though of course she couldn't understand at all. But being French, she wouldn't pry. "Julien is talking with Andrew." Elise volunteered the information. "Because he knew Thomas so well."

"Of course. I believe that's why he wants to talk with me, as well."

Camille had been involved in a relationship with Thomas for several years, though that was long ago. Elise thought Julien must be getting desperate if he was reaching that far back into the past. "Surely there must be people they could talk to who spent time with him more recently?" she asked.

Camille shrugged. "Well, he's speaking with Andrew, isn't he?"

Elise shuddered and shook her head. "I mean ... yes, I see." She slouched down on the bench.

"Don't be so worried." Camille put her hand around Elise's shoulders in a gesture of support that Elise sorely needed. They were acquaintances, really, not close friends, but they had gotten to know each other over the past few years. Single women of the same age with similar interests, in a small town, that wasn't surprising. Though Elise had spoken less frequently with Camille since Camille had started dating Sebastien. Andrew seemed to get along well with him, but he wasn't someone Elise preferred to spend time with.

Camille's eyes shifted from the door to Julien's office to the station's entrance, her lips bunched as she chewed on them, her deep red lipstick rubbing away in pale patches.

"I am sorry for your loss." Elise said. "I know it had been a few years, but you and Thomas were close. I'm sure this is distressing for you."

Camille shrugged and offered a small smile. "It had been a few years, it's true, but he was a good man." Tears gathered in her eyes. "I didn't think it would affect me so much, but ..." She waved a hand. "And of course I cannot talk with Sebastien about this."

Elise shuddered again. "No, I see." And she did see. Sebastien was not the type of man to accept that his girlfriend had ever been with another man. And certainly not a man like Thomas. Elise grinned at the thought, but changed her expression quickly when Camille's eyebrows went up. "Sorry, I was just thinking about something ..."

Camille certainly had a type. To some, Sebastien's anger and aggression made him the polar opposite of Thomas, sullen and staid. But Elise knew Thomas well enough to know that both men shared that anger, even though Thomas was better at hiding it. She'd seen his emotions flare at unexpected times, and his willingness to take it out on whoever happened to be near. Or happened to be vulnerable. What made Camille choose such men?

"He was older than me," Camille was speaking again, almost to herself. "I always knew it was a risky relationship. But I never thought he'd die ... like this ..."

The glass door swung open as Sebastien entered with a flourish. He must have come from around the building, for Elise would have seen him if he'd approached from the front drive.

"Nice trouble you've gotten into," he sneered, pushing

the sleeves of his denim jacket higher up his arms. He was dressed as he always was on his days off, when not wearing the oil-stained overalls. Blue jeans, denim jacket, hair slicked back like an icon from an American movie from the fifties. Elise had no idea where he'd developed this sense of style, but it certainly matched his attitude. Always ready for a fight, that one, with anyone, anywhere.

He dropped onto the bench next to Camille and she flinched. "I'm sorry, Seb. Chief Roche asked me to come. To talk about ..." her voice faltered.

"To talk about your old flame, right? Of course, your old man. Thought he was going to take care of you, didn't you?" His laughed grated on Elise's ears and she stood to move away. "What a fool you were, to waste yourself on an old man like that."

Camille looked down at her hands, folded in her lap. "Seb, you know he means nothing to me now."

"No?" Sebastien leaned forward, put a hand under her chin and lifted her face until her eyes met his. "Then why are you crying?"

He dropped his hand and stood, pacing around the small space.

"Seb, listen to me." Camille stood as well. "I have to answer their questions, that's all. A man is dead. Everyone is upset, aren't they?"

Elise was glad to hear Camille defend herself, though her tone remained deferential. Sebastien merely shrugged but kept pacing.

Camille waited a moment, then spoke again. "I'll come find you when I'm done, okay? I had to take the whole day off work anyway, so I'll find you."

Sebastien finally stopped pacing. "Fine. Do that." He

stepped close to her, put his hand behind her head, and kissed her forcefully. Elise turned away in embarrassment. "Find me." He said as he left the station.

11

FINDING the Bonnet house was easy. Finding Monsieur Bonnet was turning out to be less so. Adam had waited until after the traditional lunch hour to visit Monsieur Bonnet at his home. He hadn't needed Margot's reminder about French schedules, he'd learned those fast enough on his own. Everything in town — everything in France, it seemed — closed down between noon and two in the afternoon. It was lunchtime, simple as that.

Unwilling to arrive at the historian's house too early, Adam had opted for a mid-afternoon visit, hoping to find the gentleman at home. Margot had assured him that the old man kept a regular schedule, walking through town pulling his rusty old shopping cart along behind him as he passed from *boulangerie* to *boucherie* to *épicerie* a few mornings a week or walking down by the river in the evenings.

The grand house stood out from others along the narrow street that led out of town, not only because it was a story taller than the rest. A pale gray stone wall ran along the front of the property, topped with decorative red and brown stones that also served as further protection from anyone thinking of climbing over. Even with his height, Adam could just see over the top if he stood on his toes, not something he was initially inclined to do.

The house was the kind of gray that looked like it used to be white, many years ago. Someone had painted the wooden trim around the door and windows and along the roofline in a cheerful red that had long since faded to the color of mud and started to peel.

Two stone steps showing the curvature of age took Adam up to the front door. He knocked, then stepped back down to the street, so as not to be in the man's face when he opened the door. He needn't have worried. The door didn't open.

Adam waited a few minutes, then knocked again, staying next to the door this time to listen for sounds from inside. He heard nothing beyond the creak of wood as a car passed by in the road, the sound of voices coming from a house two doors up the street, a baby crying somewhere in the distance. If Monsieur Bonnet was at home, he was being very silent indeed.

Adam stepped back to eye the stone wall. It ran along the sidewalk, beyond what looked like the edge of the house. Adam followed it and saw that while the wall ran on unbroken, a second house stood behind it just past Bonnet's. Whoever lived here had taken more care of their home — the newer age of the home couldn't explain away the stark contrast in the white walls, freshly painted shutters, neatly trimmed tree branches that hung low over the wall. Even the wall seemed cleaner here, some kind of glass in the red and brown stones that topped the wall glistened in the afternoon sun.

Adam retraced his steps, beyond Monsieur Bonnet's house, and followed the wall around a corner, along a

narrow paved road. Weeds sprouted from cracks in the
pavement and along the edge, indicating that few people
drove or walked down this street. An opening in the wall
ahead on the right was partly covered by a gate that hung
loosely on its hinges. A lock darkened with age dangled
unused from one gate.

Adam stopped again to listen, and this time heard movement from beyond the gate. He pushed at it gently, calling
out as he did so. "Monsieur Bonnet? Hello?"

The sound of clay pots crashing to the ground drew his
attention to what appeared to be an old barn, just inside the
gate to his left. The door stood ajar and Adam could see the
light shifting as whoever was inside moved around. He took
a step closer and called out again. "Hello? *Bonjour?*"

Another crash, slightly smaller, preceded the barn door
swinging a bit more open. A grizzled face appeared through
the gap and eyed Adam suspiciously. "*Que'est-que c'est?
Qui etes-vous?*" What is it? Who are you?

The man's voice was low and gravelly and he spoke
with a strong accent tinged with the long, slow pronuncia-
tions common in the south of France.

"Monsieur Bonnet? *Je m'appelle Adam Kaminski.* My
name is Adam Kaminski. I was hoping to take a few
moments of your time to talk with you."

Bonnet's eyebrows shot up in an expression of open
surprise and he stepped out of the barn. The rest of him
looked exactly as Adam had expected, given what he'd seen
of the head. Smudges of dirt patterned his olive corduroy
trousers while something darker, oil perhaps, had left stains
along the cuffs of his woolen shirt. He raised a gloved hand
as if in greeting, then dropped it just as suddenly, huffed,
and walked back into the barn.

Adam stepped closer to peer into the dark interior.

Bonnet had returned to the task at hand, which appeared to be moving a large pile of empty flower pots from one side of the barn to the other, to join an even larger pile of gardening accoutrements. Pots, buckets, watering cans all piled on top of more. Adam could just make out a rake, trowel and spade slowly being buried in the mess.

Looking over his shoulder to the yard, Adam wondered why the man was keeping them all. The garden still had the bones of what had once been a formal layout, but now lay covered in dead leaves and weeds, brown stalks of plants bending toward the graveled path that ran from the barn to the back of the big house. Someone had cared for this garden once, but not anymore.

He turned his attention back to Bonnet. *"Monsieur Bonnet, parlez-vous Anglais?"* Do you speak English, he asked hopefully.

Bonnet shrugged and grunted. Adam took that as a yes.

"I'm here because I'm interested in learning something about this town's history, and I understand you're the best person to talk to about that."

That, at least, seemed to get his attention. He kept his back to Adam but stood straighter, a dented metal pot dangling from one hand. The scents of overripe soil, rotting leaves and diesel were almost overpowering.

Adam continued. "I'm particularly interested in the time around the war. About some people who lived here then."

Now Bonnet turned to face him, and Adam could see a glimmer in his eyes that hadn't been there before. "You want to talk about the resistance?" His accent in English was heavy but easily understood, almost comical by how much it sounded like a classic French accent.

"Maybe. I'm not sure. I'm looking for someone."

"Aha. Tracing the past. Good, good ..." Bonnet dropped the pot he held without looking to see where it fell and moved closer to Adam. "Tell me, are you a writer?"

"No," Adam admitted reluctantly. "I'm just interested in my own family's history."

"I see." Bonnet nodded once. "It was a long time ago."

"Yes. But I think you can help me."

Bonnet gestured with his head for Adam to follow and walked out to the garden. He stood with his back to the house, looking past the barn. "That was a difficult time." He glanced at Adam. "This part of the country was Vichy." He spat out the word as if it were a curse. And in his mind perhaps it was.

"Yes, I've heard that. I'm looking for someone — a man, I think — who was a school teacher here. At that time. I don't know if he was involved in the resistance or not."

"Not involved?" Bonnet's brow lowered. "Then I would know nothing." He looked at Adam suspiciously. "This was your family member?"

Adam shook his head. "No, my great-grandfather was a teacher in Poland. I understand he had some contact with a teacher here. In this town. I'm not sure why."

Bonnet's face contorted and he spat at Adam, a glistening lump of saliva dribbling onto the gravel at his feet. "Your family was official, then. Part of the regime."

He spun around and marched toward the house, his rolling gait revealing the pain he must have felt from such a sudden move.

"No, no, not like that." Adam walked after him. "He wasn't part of the government."

"No?" Bonnet stopped but didn't turn around.

"Well ... that is ... I'm trying to find out. I don't know

exactly what roles they played. I just have suspicions. A few clues, that's all."

Bonnet shuffled around to look at him now and his eyes glistened with excitement. "Aha, a mystery. Then I can find out — expose another collaborator, perhaps?" He lifted one lip in a lopsided grin. Or perhaps a sneer.

"Maybe," Adam hesitated. "But I suspect they may have been part of the resistance."

"Pah. If they had been, I would know of them." He paused. "What was the name?"

"Kaminski. Witold Kaminski."

"He was French?" Bonnet asked in surprise.

"No, he was Polish. A teacher. And he had connections with a local teacher, here, in this town. They exchanged letters."

"I see ... oh, I see." Bonnet shook his head and turned back toward the house muttering. "Oh yes, I shall expose him, then. They will all get what they deserve. Like that Lefebvre boy."

Adam watched helplessly as Bonnet pulled himself up the few steps to the back of the house and slammed the door behind him.

That had not gone as Adam had hoped.

He turned his back on the house and his glance followed the path of the gravel as it led beyond the barn toward a set of cement steps. Five steps led up, though Adam couldn't see more through the heavy branches that drooped from the squat trees that grew beyond the barn. He followed the path, the concrete of the steps broken and barely visible through the weeds. At the top of the steps, he stopped. He stood facing a metal wire fence. Beyond the fence, he could see another garden, this one neat and orderly. A small house stood in the center of the garden, a few potted plants decorated a small patio that held a table and three chairs.

Someone else lived there. Enjoyed sitting outside in the evening, perhaps. On land that had once been connected to Bonnet's by these steps. Why had they been cut off? What were they trying to keep in? Or keep out?

12

————

THE BREEZE PICKED up as the sun settled lower into the sky and Adam pulled his scarf tighter around his throat as he crossed *Rue Nationale*, glad the path back to his hotel kept him on the sunny side of the street. He'd handled that badly. Clearly. He stopped and leaned into the building to his right as a woman came toward him, the sidewalk not wide enough for them both to pass.

Moving on again, he replayed the conversation in his mind, each time coming up with the responses he should have offered at the time, responses that would comfort Monsieur Bonnet, help him understand that Adam was only seeking answers and that he harbored no support for the past, vicious regime.

He'd have to try again. Perhaps Margot would join him this time. She could explain to Bonnet that Adam meant no harm. His intentions were good.

That old saying about good intentions niggled at the back of his mind as he stepped closer in from the road as a large truck passed, shaking the windows in a house built along the narrow sidewalk. The road to hell is paved with good intentions.

He meant no harm, certainly, but what did he really know about his great-grandfather? Everyone else seemed to think he was a Nazi collaborator. Maybe he was. But those letters he'd found in Bermuda ...

"Mr. Kaminski!"

Adam stopped short, face to face with Elise and a young man who could only be her brother. They shared the same erect build, the same high cheekbones and generous mouth, the same worried expression in their eyes.

"Elise, sorry I didn't see you. My mind was elsewhere."

"I could tell. Andrew, this is the American I mentioned to you, Adam Kaminski. Mr. Kaminski, my brother Andrew."

"Please, call me Adam." He shook hands with the young man, who offered a quick smile just as quickly replaced with downcast eyes. "Where are you two off to?"

Elise stifled a laugh. "Forgive me. We've been here too long. I forgot that it's typical in America to ask people about their lives. We're just heading home."

Not fully understanding what she'd found humorous, Adam continued. "Tough day?"

"What makes you ask that?"

"Just used to reading people, I guess. Hazard of the job."

Andrew finally perked up at that. "The job?"

"I thought I mentioned it." Elise picked at her scarf. "Adam is a detective. In America."

Andrew seemed to shrink, his shoulders slumping inwards, and took a step back. "Where?"

"I live in Philadelphia," Adam responded. He was used to people reacting oddly when they found out he was a cop.

"Come on, I'll walk you home." Adam turned to join her, continuing back the way he had come.

"Oh, but don't you—"

"I have nowhere special to be," Adam cut her off. "In fact, I'm glad I ran into you. I could really use your help."

"My help? How?"

Adam launched into an explanation of his quest — from the first inklings that his great-grandfather had some underhanded reason for leaving Poland to his latest discovery in Bermuda. "I found letters, you see, that had been intercepted."

"From whom? And what did they say?"

Andrew's question surprised Adam. He'd been focusing on Elise, glad to see that his tale had garnered her complete attention, hopefully distracting her from dismal thoughts about the local death.

"It's not entirely clear. I think they were written in code. The folks at Bermuda Station thought so, too. On the surface, they looked like casual letters between friends. But there's no way these two were friends — how could they have ever met? No ... they were communicating something. And I want to find out what."

"So how can I help?" Elise asked.

"I tried to talk to Monsieur Bonnet just now. To see if he knew this other teacher. It didn't go well."

Elise laughed, all tension at least temporarily gone from her shoulders. "Yes, I could have warned you about him. Not an easy man to talk to, I'm afraid."

"No. I figured that out." Adam grimaced at the memory. "But maybe you can help change his mind about me?"

Elise shrugged and glanced at Adam out of the corner of her eye. "Perhaps. Of course, you may not like what he tells you."

Adam shoved his hands in his pockets. "I get that. I'm used to digging out the truth, whatever it might be. I want to do that now as well."

"Truth. Hm." Elise kept her eyes on the pavement in front of them. "I think we could all use some of that right about now."

———

ELISE PAUSED as they reached the corner. From where they stood, they could see the town square just ahead, umbrellas still set out over tables at the café despite the lateness of the year. As long as the weather held, the French would always prefer to spend time outside, enjoying the sun and the gentle breeze that drifted through the valley, watching the life of the village. To their left, the road stretched for a few hundred yards before turning toward the river, her house standing at the bend in the road. She allowed herself the pride she always felt when she saw it, tall, well kept, comfortable.

Adam must have followed her gaze because he asked, "Do you live above the café?"

Elise nodded but her intended response was cut off when Andrew chimed in, "Listen, sis, I'll see you at home later, right? I gotta go ..." he waved a hand vaguely and jogged across the street.

"Was it something I said?" Adam asked Elise with a smile.

She shook her head. "He had some interaction with the police back in Baltimore." She raised an eyebrow at Adam. "It wasn't a positive experience, to say the least. And now with this new investigation ..." her voice faltered. "And yes, to answer your question, we live above the café. We are on the second floor — what you would call the third floor."

Adam looked up. The windows of the third floor were clean, with bright red geraniums dangling over the edges of black window boxes. He looked back at Elise.

"Do you want to talk about it?" he asked, then added when he saw the confusion in her eyes, "What happened in Baltimore, I mean."

Elise laughed out loud. "Again, I always forget how forward Americans are."

Adam laughed as well, and she felt a flicker of emotion at the sparkle in his eyes and the way his dimples deepened with his laughter. She took a step closer to him and answered in a low voice. "We moved here seventeen years ago. It wasn't easy."

Adam looked down at her, but didn't speak, waiting for her to continue. "Come," she said, "come inside and I'll tell you."

He followed her as she unlocked the door of the café and she felt the warmth of his touch as he placed a hand against her back. She pulled two glasses and a bottle of wine from the armoire along the wall, then gestured for him to join her at a table in the window. This was her favorite table. From here, she could still see down to the square, watch the villagers passing through, stopping to chat, gossip and laugh. She could see the sky turning pink over the dip in the land where the river ran.

She tasted her wine as she explained her story to the man she hoped would be a friend. Perhaps more than a friend.

"Our parents died when we were still young," she said. "I was of age, old enough to be on my own. But Andrew wasn't. Almost, but not quite. I was fortunate to find good legal help. I was allowed to become his guardian."

She'd raised him, she explained, even though he was only six years younger than her. And it had been fine, at first. She was already working at that point, as a personal assistant to a local businessman. For a few years, they'd been fine. Andrew had finished high school, started a job at a local sporting goods store, even signed up to take a few night classes at the community college.

She took a sip of wine and looked out at the darkening square.

"Then something happened," Adam said. "Then the police got involved."

She laughed softly and nodded her agreement. "He was accused of killing a man."

The shift in Adam's expression was subtle, but she saw it. An eyebrow raised, a lip lowered. He took a drink of wine and said nothing, but she could feel him judging her. Judging them.

"He didn't do it, you know that," she spoke quickly, wanting his approval.

"Tell me about it," was all he said.

She shook her head as she spoke, at the memories that refused to fade. "A man was killed outside a bar. In a fight, the police thought. He was beat up pretty bad, but one of the blows had been fatal."

"Were any weapons used?" Adam asked.

Elise looked up in surprise.

"Old habits die hard, sorry," Adam put a hand out and covered hers as it lay on the table between them. "Go on."

She smiled and didn't move her hand. "Yes, but they were never found. Not a gun, you see, some kind of heavy item, like a bat, or something like that." She shrugged. "The police weren't sure. But Andrew had been there. At the bar that night. And had even spoken to the man who was killed." She took a deep breath. "He was only nineteen. He shouldn't have been there at all."

"But you're here. Both of you," Adam said. "Did they find the killer?"

Elise shook her head no. "The case was never solved. They questioned Andrew, they talked to other people, they gathered evidence." Her eyes widened as she spoke, reflecting the lack of esteem in which she held the Baltimore police.

"Why did you come here?" Adam asked.

The journey was still a blur in her mind. She wasn't really sure how they had found themselves in this beautiful land of their ancestors, where green and slate blue hills provided picture-perfect backdrops to the small towns sheltered in their vales. Something about the age of the towns, the narrow streets and solid buildings had comforted her, made her feel safe and secure.

She could still remember, as if it were yesterday, coming across the town in the early morning light. They were driving the car they had rented from the train station. They drove south, not really knowing where they were going, just knowing they needed to find somewhere to lose themselves, not to be found.

They passed larger towns with populations that would have absorbed them. And that might have worked. But none of them spoke to her, none felt just right.

Then they found this, the tiny town of *Saint-Honoré*. It had come into view suddenly, appearing before them as they came around a turn in the road, the early morning fog still rising from the ground. The town itself seemed to be ascending from the earth, the mud-brick walls floating on a cushion of mist.

They had stopped where they were, in the middle of the road, and stared at the vision before them. Slowly, carefully, they had made their way into town, not quite sure what they were looking for. But as they walked through the narrow streets and touched the old brick and stone buildings still damp from the morning air, she had known this was their new home.

She shrugged. "We had to get away. We would never have been able to move beyond that, not in Baltimore. I couldn't ..." She shuddered and picked up her glass. It was empty, so she reached over and poured another for herself and topped off Adam's. "I can't go through that again. You understand?"

He watched her, not speaking. She waited, her nerves tearing her apart. She really couldn't go through that again. But she also needed to know that someone else was responsible for Thomas' death. Someone else, not Andrew.

"So we can help each other?" She gave up waiting and spoke again.

"How can I help you?" Adam asked, his voice soft but firm. "I'm not a cop here, I can't get involved."

"You can!" She spoke urgently. "I can help you with your research. I know the townspeople, they trust me... now. And you can help me. You can prove that Andrew wasn't involved in Thomas' death. Before the police start asking more questions. Before the village turns against us." She shuddered again at the thought.

When they had arrived in this town those years ago, Elise and Andrew had rented rooms in a small and dark house, near the edge of town. It was the best they could afford with the meager savings they had between them.

Finding work was difficult. They weren't supposed to be there, they had no papers. It was easier for Andrew at first. He did manual labor, working in Thomas' farm and finding several part-time jobs from the various small farms in the region.

It had been harder for her. Although she spoke the language, she did so haltingly, trying to remember her classes from high school. She managed to find some domestic work, then she served behind the counter in a small grocery.

For a few years, they lived on edge, always waiting for that knock on the door, a police officer telling them the Baltimore murder case had been reopened, the hand on the shoulder as they walked through town on market day as they were instructed to return to the States. But as the years passed, they relaxed their watch. They began to believe they had really escaped. They began to live their lives again.

As time passed, they became a familiar part of the town. They learned not only the language, but the way of life. People stopped wondering where they had come from, and instead invited them into their homes and their lives. Elise and Andrew became part of the daily lives of the people of *Saint-Honoré*. They were kind and generous, and she would always be grateful to them for that.

Eventually, she became manager of the café, and when the elderly couple who owned it retired, she took over the business on her own. She became fully part of community life, joining the other women to knit in the evenings, meeting with them to discuss life and work. She hadn't realized until now how much that meant to her, how much the friendship and love of the town supported her.

Adam put his hand out once more, his eyes reflecting

concern but not agreement. "I want to help you, I do. And I appreciate that I really need your help."

He pulled his hand back as he shook his head and looked out the window. The town square was emptying now, villagers heading home for dinner. He downed the last of his wine and stood. Elise heard the familiar sounds of Henri getting to work in the kitchen.

"I'll see what I can do, Elise. I'll keep my eyes open, maybe find out what I can. But please understand," he interrupted her as she stood to thank him. "I make no promises. There's really not much I can do."

"Thank you." She felt her hand shake, tears coming to her eyes. "Thank you."

13

THE SCENT of tobacco lingered in the coats of the men who gathered around the front door of the *tabac* between drinks and wafted in each time the door opened. Smoking wasn't permitted within the establishment, but that didn't seem to dim their enjoyment of it.

Nico's *tabac* looked different in the evening. Men gathered in clumps around the two tall stools in front of the darkened wood bar, leaning into each other as they spoke in low voices. Each time a newcomer entered, he would be greeted by everyone else — they all seemed to know each other — though kissed on the cheeks by only a handful of closer friends.

Everyone except Adam, that was. He caught a few sideways glances as he returned, even a nod from one customer, but not broad smiles or hellos. Even Andrew, who stood in one of the clumps around the bar, simply nodded a greeting but nothing more.

"Detective, did you find what you were looking for?" Nico stepped up close behind him, his quiet voice making his accent even harder to understand.

"I did, thank you for your help." Adam turned and followed Nico with his gaze as the bartender worked his way back around to his side of the bar. "Water, please," he answered to Nico's questioning gaze.

Adam took a drink then turned and leaned against the bar, checking out the rest of the place.

The few tables at the back of the room stood empty. Most of the men at the bar had beers, a handful drank wine. One young man downed a shot of a clear liquid. And slammed it back onto the bar a little too forcefully. Adam's muscles tensed and he put his glass back down. He recognized the young man as the aggressive mechanic who'd accosted him before.

The mechanic was the only person there speaking loudly, his voice carrying throughout the room. Every now and then, Andrew would put a hand on his arm, as if to quiet him, but it served no purpose. Adam couldn't understand him, despite the volume, as his words slurred together when he talked.

But other men around him clearly understood him and occasionally grimaced, occasionally flinched in response. The grumpy old man Adam had encountered that morning, and now knew to be Enzo, glared toward Sebastien with every outburst.

"Sebastien, keep quiet, you're being a fool." Nico called to him, then walked over to refill his empty glass and wipe the bar down in front of him.

"Me? Why do you care? Oh, because of him." Sebastien glared at Adam. "Should I be careful what I say in front of the American?" he continued in English.

Adam raised an eyebrow, but didn't respond. Sebastien slid down the bar toward him anyway, wobbling unsteadily. "Nico thinks I should be careful what I say around you."

"I couldn't understand you, anyway, so I don't think you need to worry." Adam looked away as he responded.

"Hmph, of course not, Mr. American. Don't speak French, do you?"

Adam shrugged and didn't take the bait.

"I said," Sebastien emphasized his words, "that my Camille is a little too upset about Thomas. I said she should pay more attention to me."

For a moment, Adam thought he'd misheard. "Thomas? The man who died?"

"Ha!" Sebastien slurped down another shot. "Yes, of course the man who died."

"Camille is Sebastien's girlfriend," Nico explained to Adam, his voice once again low. "She had a relationship with Thomas, in the past."

"Ah." Adam watched Sebastien as he fiddled with his shot glass, turning it this way and that. "I see."

"No you don't see." Sebastien turned on him. "Why should I put up with that from her?"

Adam stared him down but didn't respond.

"Hmph," Sebastien waved to Nico for another shot. "I have half a mind to beat that out of her."

Adam's tension returned. Andrew laughed into his beer, though Adam didn't think there was anything funny about the threat.

"Ignore him," Nico said as he refilled Sebastien's glass. "He doesn't mean it."

"The young don't know what it really means to be French anymore," Enzo chimed in, surprising Adam with the quality of his English. "They think like Americans, not about the past only about the quick dollar."

Sebastien downed his drink, slamming the glass down

again. He turned suddenly, lunging toward Enzo, who stepped backwards to avoid him.

"*Fascaga!*"

Adam moved quickly, wrapping one strong arm under Sebastien's arms and pushing him back against the bar. He couldn't tell if he was holding Sebastien back or holding him up.

He looked to Andrew for help. Andrew simply shrugged. "*Ne t'attache pas, ne t'implique pas.*" Don't get attached, don't get involved. Great.

Adam growled under his breath but turned back to Sebastien. "You've had too much, you're going to hurt someone. Probably yourself."

He gave Andrew one more look, then wrapped a strong arm around Sebastien's shoulders. "Come on, man, I'll walk you out." It might have looked like a friendly gesture, but years of experience on the Philadelphia police force, coupled with Adam's size, meant the movement was not optional. Sebastien resisted but moved along with Adam.

"Hold on." Andrew downed the last of his beer and stood. "I'll make sure he gets home."

Sebastien spluttered but complied. He threw Adam a nasty glare as he was escorted out of the *tabac*.

Nico shrugged, wiping his hands on the white towel. "You've not made a friend there."

"Should I be worried?"

"No, he's harmless. Mostly." He smiled. "Come, relax. Have some wine and let me tell you about our town."

———

THE GLASS of wine that Nico poured out for Adam almost glowed in the dim light, a dark, ruby red. Adam saw the glint in Nico's eye as he waited for Adam to taste it, so he complied, offering what he hoped were intelligent comments on the taste and smell. Wine expert, he was not. Give him a good whiskey any day of the week. But he did his best.

"Nice," he rubbed his lips together as if considering the taste. "Well balanced, not too sweet or too dry."

Nico nodded, a broad smile on his face. "That is just a taste of what I will be producing soon."

"This is your wine?" Adam asked, surprised. He took another taste. "That's really good."

"Well, it's not really my wine," Nico shrugged, looking down as he dragged a cloth along the bar. Enzo, who had settled onto one of the only tall stools available, snorted. Nico glared at him, but continued. "That is a blend of grapes from a number of local wineries, including mine."

"Yours!" Enzo grunted out the word with a laugh.

"Mine and Thomas'," Nico added with another glance at Enzo. "We invested together, we have been working on the vineyard. It has some very good potential."

"Your wine, hah!" Enzo interjected again, this time leaning toward the two men. "You couldn't make good wine. You wouldn't know good wine if you drowned in it. Only Thomas had the skill, the taste. You have nothing without him. Pah." Enzo grunted and turned back to the bar, worn out, perhaps, from this energetic display.

"Enzo here," Nico explained with a touch of sarcasm in his voice, "is our local wine expert." He added, muttering under his breath, "And Thomas wasn't the great person Enzo seems to think he was."

"Oh really?" Adam asked.

"Enzo works as the estate manager at the big estate." Nico gestured over his shoulder as he spoke, perhaps imagining the hills that rose gently behind the town covered in a patchwork of vines.

"Vines are better on the hill, in that soil," Enzo mumbled into his drink. "It is the *terroir* that makes the wine. Thomas understood, he understood grapes."

Adam watched the grizzled old man for a moment before turning back to Nico. Keeping his voice low, he asked, "Does he really manage a large estate?"

"It does not seem possible, does it? But yet, he still does. His family ran that estate in years past, now they manage it for the new owners. He does not look like much, but I suppose they keep him on as a favor to the family."

Adam couldn't be sure, but he though he saw Enzo grin. Had he heard their whispered conversation? Did he care?

As if reading his thoughts, Enzo turned his head just enough to catch Adam's eye. And he winked.

Then he returned his focus to his drink and let out an unintelligible growl.

What the hell was wrong with these people? Adam actually laughed out loud.

"Adam? What is it?" Nico asked.

"Sorry," Adam shook his head and finished his wine. It really was good, even though he was no expert. He could get used to this. "Is everyone in this town so miserable to strangers?"

Nico smiled. "I am working on that, you see. I wish to put our town on the tourist map. To bring in more Americans," he gestured to Adam. "We want to welcome strangers. To invite them to visit our town, drink our wine, buy our food and stay in our hotels."

"*Putain!*" Enzo actually shouted. "Why would you bring that down upon our heads?"

Nico dropped his rag onto the bar and turned to Enzo,

hands on his hips. "You do not know, old man. We need to bring this town back to life or we will die off, like all the other old towns."

"We will never die," Enzo mumbled, then continued in rambling French that Adam couldn't follow.

Nico could, and responded in kind, his anger sometimes getting the better of him, sometimes receding in a wave of disgust toward the old man.

Adam watched the two men bickering. It was an important question, no doubt. Was it wise to encourage tourism to a little town like *Saint-Honoré*? Would it help revive the town or hasten its demise?

But these were not the questions Adam was here to answer. As fascinating as the topic was, it would neither resolve the truth about Adam's great-grandfather nor produce a solution to his newest puzzle, the death of Thomas Lefebvre. On the other hand ... Adam glanced out the door, picturing Sebastien staggering out, one arm around the shoulder of his neighbor. That young man certainly raised some questions in Adam's mind.

14

<hr/>

"THAT BOY," Elise muttered under her breath as she hurried back toward the café. She knew Henri and Helene were fine on their own this evening. It would be a slow night, no doubt, with most of the town gossiping in the *tabac*, trying to pick up the latest news about Thomas' death. But surely Andrew could have stayed to help her. Or at least could have stayed so she knew where he was. She'd finally given up waiting and gone out to find him, leaving her chef and waitress on their own. She'd arrived just in time to see him practically carrying Sebastien out of the bar, Adam watching from the doorway. She'd paused, then retraced her steps. She didn't want anything to do with a drunk Sebastien.

"Madame, please!"

She pulled up short but not before bumping into Philippe Bonnet, knocking herself almost off balance.

"I'm so sorry, Monsieur Bonnet, my mind was elsewhere."

"As were your eyes," the old man added unkindly. He

bent down to straighten his trousers and she noticed the bright yellow flowers of the *chélidoine* weed that grew along the riverbank clinging to his ankles, the red mud of the river on his shoes.

"Out for an evening walk?" she asked, trying to change the mood of the conversation.

"Yes, of course." He finished wiping down his pants and straightened to look at her. "Every day, as you know. We must enjoy the pleasures we have available to us. While we still can."

"Oh, Monsieur Bonnet, you are too hard on yourself." She moved a hand as if to touch his shoulder, then pulled it back seeing the look in his eyes. "You torture yourself over your research. I'm glad that you can enjoy yourself, take pleasure from our beautiful town. And I have no doubt that you will continue to do so for many years to come."

"Spoken with the ignorance of youth," he frowned as he spoke, but Elise knew this was one of his favorite topics and didn't mind. She was also at a point in her life when she didn't mind being called young.

"My research is too important to take lightly. We must always remember the past, we must dig out the truth. And," his eyes sparkled, "we must hold the guilty accountable."

"And give credit to those who fight the good fight, don't you agree?" she asked, raising a finger to stop his flow of words.

"What? Oh," he stuttered. "Of course. But we all know who fought on the side of right, don't we?"

Elise shrugged, keeping her voice light. "There's an American in town, Adam Kaminski." Bonnet's brows dropped and a low grumble seemed to come from this throat, so Elise continued quickly. "His ancestor may have been part of the resistance, you know. Fighting against the Nazis from Poland, doing what he could."

"Why do you think that," Bonnet frowned as he spoke, but there was a quickening of interest in his tone.

"Why?" Elise thought quickly. "Because Adam himself is a good person. Because he took the time and money to come here to find the truth. Because I believe it must be true."

Bonnet threw his head back and laughed. "That is no reason, and you know it." He took a moment to compose himself. "But I agree, we must side with the survivors. We must help those who remain, even as we punish those responsible."

Elise watched the indecision move across his face, then he nodded. "I will look into his past, as he asked. But remember," he held up a finger of his own this time, "I will not hide the truth from him. Whatever it may be."

"You are a good man, Monsieur Bonnet." Elise leaned forward and pecked him on the cheek before he could resist. He grumbled again and shuffled away, still swiping at the petals that clung to his trousers.

Elise laughed to herself as she watched him go. Her good mood didn't last, however. As she came to the turn in the road that exposed the town square, she saw Camille sitting alone on a bench.

"*Bon soir*, Camille. It is a beautiful evening, is it not?" Elise perched on the bench next to Camille. When Camille smiled and nodded, she slid back more comfortably.

"I suppose it is," Camille's words were in agreement but her tone conveyed a different sentiment.

"Are you waiting for Sebastien?" Elise asked, thinking Camille might not yet be aware of his condition. The bench on which they sat commanded a view of the town square, but from an angle Elise rarely stopped to appreciate. From here, it was clearly more of a triangle than a square, with streets stretching out away from town like fingers reaching out to the hills, the vineyards, the farms.

"Waiting for Sebastien, yes," Camille said. "But not waiting for him to come here." She glanced at Elise, then glanced as quickly away. "He just needs some time to himself."

"Ah," Elise understood exactly. She'd seen Sebastien in one of his "moods" as the townspeople called them. Drunken rages, more like.

She considered the woman sitting next to her, wondering what made women — herself no exception— make some truly bad choices at times. Camille was a beautiful woman, full figured with a pretty smile and perfect blue eyes. Why would she settle with Sebastien? For that matter, why had she settled for Thomas previously, a man more than a few years older than her?

"I can't imagine Sebastien is sad that Thomas is dead," she said aloud.

Camille glared at her, and she immediately apologized. "I don't mean to make light of the situation, I'm sorry, either of Sebastien's anger or Thomas' death."

Camille took a breath and looked back over the square. "Who knows what's going through anyone's mind?" was her only response.

Elise could only agree silently to that. It really was a beautiful evening. The weather was unseasonably warm for October, and she sat in only a cardigan over her dress with no discomfort.

After a few moments of silence, Camille spoke again. "It's true, of course. Sebastien hated Thomas. For no good reason." She slammed one fist into the other. "My relationship with Thomas was over long before I started spending time with Sebastien."

Elise nodded, willing her to continue. Which she did.

"But his temper ... well, you know."

Elise nodded once more, adding. "I do know. I've also seen how good he can be to you." She wasn't lying so much as stretching the truth. Sebastien was clearly smitten with Camille, in his own way. The way he watched her as he walked, the way he smiled when she approached him. Even the way he smacked her on the bottom, his own gesture of affection. She wondered if Camille saw it that way.

"Are you happy with Sebastien? Do you trust him?" she asked.

Camille lifted one shoulder and turned her lips down. "Happy? Who can say? As happy as I could be with any man from this town, I suppose."

"There are other men. Other towns."

"Perhaps. But where would I go? What would I do?"

"You work in a shop," Elise said. "You can do that anywhere. I'm sure you could find work."

Camille's eyes narrowed but she smiled as she said, "Are you trying to get rid of me, Mademoiselle Martin?"

Elise laughed. "Of course not, I hope you stay right here in *Saint-Honoré*, and find a man who will make you truly happy."

Camille laughed too, then stopped abruptly and stood. "I've said too much, wasted too much time. I must find Sebastien and bring him home. He'll be wanting something to eat."

Elise shook her head as she watched her friend walk away. How little we really know about each other, when we are forced to think about it. She had no doubt that Sebastien could have killed Thomas. But what about Camille. Did that quiet woman hide secrets of her own?

She laughed at the thought, then chastised herself. She shouldn't go around suspecting her own friends. She knew the time might come when she would need all the friends she could get.

15

ADAM FOLLOWED an indirect path from the *tabac* to his hotel, wandering through the town's narrow streets, few though they were. He had no pressing business back at the hotel — and calling it a hotel was stretching it a bit, anyhow. A house that let out a few rooms, that was all. But owned by a friendly couple — the friendliest people he'd met in town so far, to be honest. Perhaps they would appreciate Nico's efforts to increase tourism to the town.

He shifted his path when he recognized the back of Margot Roche as she stopped to peer in a shop window.

"Looking for new curtains?" he asked lightly.

She almost jumped at the sound of his voice and her face was startled as she turned to him, but shifted to a friendly smile when she recognized him. "Ah, that inquisitiveness, it is so American."

"Right, sorry." Adam still couldn't get the hang of blending in around here. He'd have to work harder at it.

"Good night," Margot said as she turned to continue her walk.

Adam stepped into place beside her. "May I join you?" He resisted asking where she was going.

She smiled and offered one nod of approval. "Of course. How are you enjoying this evening?"

"It's been interesting so far." He laughed. "You have some fascinating characters in this town."

"We certainly do," Margot's mouth twitched as if trying to hide her smile. "Who have you met?"

"Just a few men at the *tabac*," Adam kept his answer vague. No need to start gossiping about Margot's neighbors. She reached her own conclusion, however.

"Ah. Interesting people at the *tabac*. I suspect you've met my uncle."

"Your uncle? I don't know, maybe I have. I met a few men."

"My married name is Margot Roche. But I was born Margot Marchand. Perhaps you recognize the name?"

Adam shook his head.

"No? Most people around here do. We were large land holders once. My family still owns a small vineyard out of town."

"Very nice," Adam murmured, wondering how to respond to a story that sounded like one of loss.

"I supposed you may have met my uncle Enzo. He is frequently to be found stirring up trouble in the *tabac*." Her words were harsh but she smiled as she said it, and for a moment Adam could see Enzo in her eyes — at least, the Enzo who had winked mysteriously before slipping back into his supposed anger.

Adam laughed at the recognition. "I surely did meet him. And interesting is, without question, the best way to describe him. Though I suspect he's more than he appears."

Margot smiled and nodded in agreement. "He manages the estate at the top of the town. He was given the position because of our family's history with wine. I admit, I'm not always sure the owner is getting what he's paying for, sadly."

"You think he can't do the job?"

"Can't? Uncle Enzo?" Now it was Margot's turn to laugh. "There is nothing that man can't do, if he puts his mind to it. But does he? Well, that's another question, isn't it?"

As they walked, Adam thought about Margot's description of Enzo, of his wink, of their past, and realized he was beginning to understand these people. In all their gruff, crotchety, unwelcoming ways.

"I just spent some time talking with Nico, learning about his winery."

"His winery?" Margot's step faltered, but she quickly resumed the rhythm of her walk. "It's a bit soon to be saying that."

"Of course, I'm sorry. Enzo said the same thing. The winery belonged to Thomas, is that right?"

"That's right," Margot sighed. "What a waste. What a loss. He was a good man, Thomas. I will miss him."

Adam noted the difference in opinion between Margot and Nico when it came to Thomas, but didn't comment on it. They walked in silence, the setting sun reflecting against the few shop windows they passed, making it impossible to see inside. Many of the buildings were of an older age, built in a thick gray stone through which no large store fronts had been cut. Placards hung from narrow doorways indicating the nature of the business inside.

"But I suppose it is Nico's winery now." Margot continued as if there had been no break in their conversation.

"Were they partners?"

"In a way. Thomas started that winery. On a small part of his lavender farm. Only a few acres at first, to test out the terroir, see what grapes would grow."

"And how did it work?"

"It must have worked well, because he planted more. Oh, I suppose it's been six years now. I know that he and Nico made some sort of arrangement early on."

"What type of arrangement?"

Margot offered a gallic shrug. "Over money, I am sure. Nico always seems to have more than anyone else. Thomas needed to increase his yield, improve his equipment, and for that, he would have needed an investor."

Adam considered this. It made perfect sense — the man who owned a local bar would be interested in investing in a local winery. But anytime money was involved, there was always a motive for murder.

"Does Nico benefit from Thomas' death?" he asked.

"I don't see how." Margot seemed honestly confused.

"Well, he owns the winery now, right?"

"I suppose. But probably not the lavender farm, which is how Thomas made most of his income. That would go to his sisters, his heirs. Plus, Thomas was the true winemaker, Nico was just an investor."

"Hm," Adam laughed gently. "Your uncle said something similar."

Margot tipped her head. "He is a wise man, in his own way."

They had reached an intersection that dictated the end of their stroll together. The narrow alley to the right would lead Margot toward her house and her waiting husband. The slightly wider street to the left would take Adam back to the main square and, just beyond that, his little hotel.

"It's a pleasure speaking with you, as usual," Adam said. "But I suspect I should be talking less about wine and more about history." And about finding a murderer, he thought to himself.

"Oh no, Monsieur Kaminski." Margot shook her head vehemently. "If you want to understand our past, then you surely must understand our town today, our culture. Just as the *terroir* makes the wine, you must understand the land to understand the people."

"That's true, everything is relevant. Though the town now isn't really the same as it was, is it?"

Margot laughed. "Of course not. It was changed by the same thing that changed everything in France. The war."

"It's such a terrible part of history, I know. The devastation and loss it caused."

"It did. My own family land was lost during the war. The land of people like the Bonnet's, once wealthy merchants. Before the war."

"It's a sad history."

"Hm, perhaps." Margot's tone wavered. "In the case of my family, or the Bonnet's for the worse. But in some ways, many ways, for the better."

"How so?"

"Some of our parents, our grandparents, our great-grandparents, some of them did the right thing. Not like the Lefebvres or Dubois. Some of them did the right thing."

"Which was?"

Margot looked up at him, a smile playing at the corner of her lips, her eyes bright. "The children, Monsieur Kaminski. They tried to save the children. And we are all the better for it."

"I don't understand."

"No? Then I will show you. Perhaps tomorrow. I will

contact you tomorrow. For now, goodnight, Monsieur Kaminski."

Adam watched her walk away, her short red hair brown in the fading light, and wondered what she had in store for him tomorrow.

16

ADAM TOOK the narrow street to the main square, but he was not eager to go back to his hotel. Perhaps dinner at Elise's café, he thought. A chance to sit down and figure out how to approach Philippe Bonnet tomorrow — and do a better job of it this time. Perhaps also a chance for some good company, he admitted to himself, picturing Elise's welcoming smile.

As he crossed the square, he caught sight of Sebastien. The young man's gate was surprisingly steady. He couldn't have worked off that much alcohol that quickly, could he? Maybe he was just used to carrying it. To posing as a sober man.

The young man carried something long in his hand, and Adam risked staring to figure out what it was. Some type of pipe, but with a knob on one end. Sebastien was a mechanic. Could he be working at this time of night? He turned to follow from a safe distance, watching to see where Sebastien went.

There were still a few people out on the street, but a small town was far from a good venue for tailing someone.

And not knowing the town, Adam couldn't risk letting Sebastien get too far ahead.

Sebastien turned into a dark street, and Adam picked up his pace to catch up. He paused before looking around the corner. Sebastien stood still, bouncing the pipe, or whatever it was, gently in his hands. As he tossed it, he looked over his shoulder. Adam pulled back behind the wall, uncertain if he'd been spotted or not. He waited for a count of ten, then looked again.

Sebastien had moved on, farther down the street. Adam waited. There were no doorways here for him to hide in, no other people on the street to block Sebastien's view. It was good he waited. Sebastien pulled open a door at the end of the block and entered. Glancing around, Adam jogged to the doorway, his heart racing. If Sebastien came out, he'd come face to face. And if Sebastien was as angry now as he'd been earlier, Adam had no doubt that would mean a fight.

Jogging up to the doorway Sebastien had entered, Adam saw the sign. *Bertrand Garage et Pièces Auto.* Auto repairs.

So he was working this late at night. Drunk. Interesting fellow.

He shook his head, turned and jogged back up to the other street before Sebastien could come out. Turning the corner at speed, he ran right into Philippe Bonnet.

"Ach!" The old man spat out. "*Monsieur, qu'est-ce que c'est?* What is going on this evening? Why is everybody running around?"

Adam pulled up short. "Monsieur Bonnet, hello. I'm so sorry. *Pardon. Je regret.*" Adam gave up using the few French words he knew to apologize. "Adam Kaminski," he added when the man looked at him blankly. "We met earlier today. At your house."

The scowl on Bonnet's face let Adam know he remembered him.

"Monsieur, please allow me to apologize."

Bonnet waved a hand to silence him. "It is not necessary. Mademoiselle Martin has explained to me."

"Elise?"

Bonnet frowned at the use of her name, but nodded. "She is sure that your search is admirable, that this ancestor you wish to learn about was part of the resistance, not supporting the Vichy." He bent forward to wipe off his trousers, which were already filthy and certainly no dirtier for Adam having run into them.

Adam hesitated. He'd like to think that was true. But was it? But he wouldn't put Elise's intervention to waste. At least Bonnet was listening now. "Yes, it's true. I was not clear earlier, when I saw you. I do want your help finding the truth about someone from the resistance. Someone who fought the Nazis." He flinched only slightly at the brazen lie. After all, it was a lie he was fervently hoping was true. Despite all the evidence to the contrary.

"Hm." A spark of interest lit the old man's eyes and he straightened his back. "Tell me more."

Adam launched into his story, keeping his speech slow so as not to lose his audience. He explained about the letters found in the Bermuda Station Hotel, letters that hinted at code, at efforts to undermine the Nazi regime, some kind of secret communication channels that were used to serve some purpose — though he didn't know what.

As he spoke, the sky gradually darkened, but Bonnet didn't seem to mind. His attention was rapt, hanging on every word of Adam's story. Clearly, this is how he should have started earlier.

Adam paused to take a breath and give Bonnet a chance

to digest what he'd said so far, when a church bell chimed. Bonnet grunted and looked at his watch.

"Enough." He held up a dirt encrusted hand. "Tomorrow. I must return home now."

He continued down the road without another word. Adam watched him go, then turned back to Elise's café and what he hoped would be a hearty dinner and a good night's sleep. For tomorrow would likely be a very interesting day.

17

"Ah, Monsieur Kaminski. Finally, I found you."

Margot caught Adam just as he'd put a forkful of scrambled egg into his mouth and he held up a hand to apologize as he finished chewing.

She laughed. "I'm sorry to interrupt your breakfast." She glanced down at his plate of eggs, Canadian bacon, brioche and coffee. A similarly laden plate sat in front of another chair, but looked untouched. "A very American breakfast, too, it looks."

Adam swallowed as he nodded. "Elise was kind enough to prepare something she knew I'd enjoy. Not that I don't love French food as well."

"That goes without saying," Margot responded with a smile as she took an empty chair at his table in Elise's café. "I was surprised when I heard I could find you here. Elise is not usually open this early in the day."

She looked around the café as she spoke. All of the other tables were empty, not even set for future diners. Silverware, plates, napkins were all neatly stacked on the sideboard that ran the length of the far wall. She jumped at a loud crash coming from the kitchen and moved as if to stand.

"Don't worry," Adam put out a hand to stop her. "It's just Andrew and Sebastien. Repairing something in the kitchen. That's where Elise is right now. She'll be back in a minute, I'm sure."

"Hmm," Margot smiled lightly and settled back into her chair.

When Elise had invited Adam for what she promised would be a typical American breakfast, he'd accepted eagerly. But Sebastien's arrival with Andrew about ten minutes after his put a damper on his enthusiasm.

The two men glared at each other as Elise rushed to welcome Sebastien and thank him for coming. She glanced warily between Adam and Sebastien as she spoke. "You are too kind to take your time to help us," she told him as she ushered him quickly through to the kitchen. "Andrew knows so much about farm equipment, but perhaps it is not exactly the same as fixing an oven."

Her voice faded as the three of them moved into the kitchen. Elise reappeared only a minute later. "I am so sorry. I have heard about your encounter with Sebastien last night. I should have thought to tell Andrew to bring him through the back door."

Adam laughed. "Don't worry, please. Are you afraid that I'll attack him?" He paused mid-laugh. "Or that he'll attack me?" He suddenly saw far less humor in it. He didn't, however, feel any surprise that Elise had already heard about the incident. He knew how fast news traveled in a small town.

"No, no ... of course not." Elise smiled, but her eyes still held that wariness Adam was getting used to from her.

"Now. My lower oven may be broken, but I can still make some mean scrambled eggs. Sound good?"

"Absolutely. And I'm looking forward to the opportunity to chat, too."

A loud bang from the kitchen interrupted their conversation, and Elise hurried back to see what was going on. Which is where she was again now. For the third time that morning. Perhaps Sebastien wasn't as good at repairs as people thought.

"Monsieur Kaminski, I have a proposition for you." Margot's words brought Adam back to the present and his cooling breakfast.

"I've been looking forward to hearing this," Adam said, then took another mouthful. "I hope you don't mind if I eat while you talk?"

"Please do." Margot waved a hand of approval over his food. "I hope Elise is back shortly as well. So," she paused and Adam realized that whatever she was about to tell him, she was pleased with herself for concocting it. "To explain, I must start with the past."

Adam choked lightly on his coffee as he laughed while taking a sip. "Of course, where else?"

Margot's smile faded, and she toyed with the edge of the table cloth. "This is not a pleasant place, this history where I am taking you."

Adam nodded, understanding that this story would start with the war. With the Vichy regime. With the Nazis. No, this wouldn't be a good place.

"You have heard, I imagine, of the *Kindertransport*?"

Adam nodded, but Margot continued nevertheless, talking as much to herself as to him. "Jewish and Quaker organizations funded a rescue effort, a kind of Underground Railroad, to help save children from the Nazis.

Thousands of children escaped Germany in the late 1930s, even early 1940s. On trains, with the help of locals in Germany. Most went to England. Some to other European countries that were not under Nazi control. The children had to go by themselves, of course. This Underground Railroad was for children only. Not for their parents."

Adam stared at his hands as she spoke. How could he not do more with these hands? He had strength, he had some level of power. Yet he felt helpless in the face of these stories of pain, loss and death.

"You may not know there was a similar network helping children escape Poland," Margot continued.

Adam looked up, surprised. "You're right, I didn't know that. What do you know of it?"

"As it turns out, quite a lot." Margot spoke with a wry smile.

Adam leaned forward in his seat, forgetting for a moment the banging still emanating from the kitchen, his and Elise's eggs growing cold and hard on their plates.

"There were many people involved in these networks. French, Poles, Jews, others who simply wanted to do something good in such a terrible, evil time." She looked him in the eye and held his gaze. "Some of these children escaped here. To *Saint-Honoré*."

"Ah, the Jewish children." Elise slid onto her chair, breaking the spell that had bound Adam's gaze so tightly to Margot's.

Margot blinked and looked away. "Elise, *bonjour*." The two woman kissed cheeks.

Elise poked at her food with her fork, frowned, then dropped the fork. "Adam, I am so sorry. I hope you had a chance to eat?" She glanced down at his half-eaten breakfast and frowned again. "Let me replace that, please." She grabbed both plates and returned to the kitchen.

Throughout the exchange, Adam hadn't removed his eyes from Margot. "Go on," he said.

She nodded, took a breath. "Most of those children are now gone, of course. Many moved on from here. This was not a safe place at that time, either. Merely a staging ground, a place where people were friendly, willing to help, but not a place where they would be safe. The Vichy regime ..." She shuddered. "They had no compassion, no concern about turning over any Jews they found."

Adam saw a glint of a tear in her eye, and looked away.

"But some stayed," she said. "Some were adopted by local families. They were raised as Catholics. As French. The young ones, those who could more easily absorb the new language, new culture, new religion."

"Are any of them still here? Still alive?" Adam asked, trying to add up the years in his head.

Margot nodded. "Yes, a few. But there are descendants. Oh yes," she smiled at Adam's look of surprise. "But of course. These children, they grew up. They had families of their own. And these — the children, the grandchildren of the rescued Jewish children, they are still here. In *Saint-Honoré*."

"That's ..." Adam coughed to clear his throat. "That's an amazing story. Thank you for sharing it."

Margot shook her head. "You don't understand. You want to learn something about your ancestor who was in Poland during the war. I am sure Monsieur Bonnet will be able to find this person, if he had any connection to *Saint-Honoré*, as you believe. But until then, I thought this would also help you. Help you understand that time. This town."

"What's that?"

"I have arranged for you to join them in a meeting. Today, at lunch."

"A meeting?" Adam asked. He heard his voice rise in surprise and coughed again to cover it up.

"Yes, they meet regularly, for lunch, coffee, drinks, you know. They are a community within our community. And they are willing to include you in their meeting today." Margot laughed. "For as many of these descendants as choose to come, choose to tell their story."

The kitchen door swung open and Elise brought out two fresh plates of food. "Now, eat," she commanded. "Don't let this one go to waste as well."

As she sat down, the kitchen door swung open again and Andrew emerged followed closely by Sebastien.

"Elise, have you seen my gloves?" Andrew leaned toward his sister, his voice low. "My brown work gloves?"

Elise shrugged. "No. Are they in the apartment?"

Andrew shook his head. "I didn't see them. I'll look again later."

Adam glanced at the young men, but returned his focus to Margot — while also taking a few bites of his fresh breakfast, of course. "Elise, Margot has arranged for me to meet some of the townspeople who have ancestors from Germany and Poland. Who were brought here during the war."

"Ah, yes. I heard you talking about them earlier."

"Ha!" All three of them looked over to where Sebastien stood by the front entrance, his coat slung casually over one shoulder.

"Something wrong?" Adam asked in a low voice.

"Don't worry, you have nothing to fear." Sebastien grinned. "But you are wasting your time, meeting with that group." He turned as if to leave, then swung back toward the group at the table. "Those old people, they think they know so much. They know what it means to be French, hah!" His laugh was harsh and grating. "We young, we understand more than they do."

Andrew gave Sebastien a look that meant nothing to Adam, but clearly conveyed something to the young mechanic. He shrugged and pulled the front door open. "Do what you want."

After the two men had left the café, Elise turned to Adam. "There are some people, like Sebastien, who think we need to move on, to let the past go."

"I can't agree with that sentiment." Adam shook his head. "I'm glad to learn more, to meet with them. But ..."

"What?" Margot asked.

"What can I offer them in return? In return for their time, I mean. For talking with me?"

"Nothing," Margot said. "Why would they need anything from you?"

Adam said nothing, focusing his attention instead of finishing the meal Elise had been kind enough to provide twice. But his mind was reeling. Why would they, indeed? Could it be because his ancestor, his great-grandfather, had somehow been complicit in causing the devastation of their lives?

18

WHAT A MESS. Elise swept up the bits of plaster and plastic that had fallen over the kitchen as Andrew and Sebastien moved, repaired and returned her oven to its place. She appreciated the free labor, no doubt, but couldn't they at least have laid a cloth down? She shook her head, let out a deep sigh, and went back to work.

After the floor, she turned her attention to the rest of the kitchen. She would open for lunch in just a few hours, and everything needed to be scrubbed before that could happen.

As she worked, she thought about Adam Kaminski. He had offered to help her and Andrew, she knew. But what did she really know about him? He'd presented himself as a cop from Philadelphia, and she'd simply accepted that statement. That wasn't like her. She wasn't usually that trusting. She was falling for him, she knew it. She had to be more careful.

She stopped mid-swipe and dropped her rag into the sink. She *wasn't* usually that trusting, and for good reason.

Her natural distrust had kept them safe for this long, it was no time to abandon it now.

Checking the kitchen to see that most of the work had been done, she flicked off the lights and ran up the back stairs that led to her private apartment. They were not rich, she and Andrew, but they had all the comforts of life she could want. Including a relatively new laptop computer and WiFi throughout her apartment and the café below.

As the computer powered on, she thought about the best terms to use to find what she needed to know. She tapped her fingers impatiently as she waited, and as soon as the search bar appeared, she wrote: "Adam Kaminski Philadelphia USA police officer."

The search produced only the fact that Adam was exactly who he claimed to be: a cop. An accomplished cop, in fact. A series of articles popped up about the high profile cases he had solved and his other accomplishments.

This was only the public information, though. Elise knew as well as anyone that everyone had private information. Details they might not want others to know.

She kept digging.

It only took twenty more minutes. Twenty minutes and a series of useless search terms followed by an avalanche of very useful terms. "Discipline" led to "probation" led to "psychological evaluation."

Elise sat reading over the psychological evaluation the City of Philadelphia had ordered on Adam Kaminski after he'd been temporarily suspended a couple of years ago. An evaluation that had been stolen in a hack of the department's computer system and ultimately posted online with other sensitive documents. Interesting reading, to say the least.

Her eyes scanned the pages first, catching on a few key

phrases: rebellious toward authority figures... impulsive behavior and sudden bursts of anger... intelligence and empathy.

She went back and read the document more thoroughly, then set it aside and leaned back in her chair. Well. That was more than she'd hoped to find. A good cop who was known to act impulsively, to break the rules when necessary.

Without knowing any of that, she'd asked him to help her, invited him into the most personal part of her life and asked him for help.

How fortuitous.

19

Adam let out an angry sigh and closed his book. There was no point, he couldn't focus. He looked around the *tabac*, then moved from his table against the wall to the bar. Getting Nico's attention, he ordered another coffee.

He was worried about meeting with these people, the descendants of the Jewish children who had escaped Poland. He could admit that to himself. But he couldn't put his finger on why, exactly, he was worried. Did he feel guilty? That was absurd. He wasn't involved in their past.

But his great-grandfather might have been. One way or another. The cause of his worry was the fact that he didn't know which way — was he someone who helped them survive? Or someone who chased them down?

He shook his head as he grabbed the coffee Nico handed him.

"You look like you need more than coffee, my friend," Nico said with a smile. "A *pastis*, perhaps?"

Adam grinned and shook his head. "A little too early for me," he replied. "But you're right, it probably would help."

Nico said nothing more, simply returning to some paperwork he had spread out over the bar.

Adam gave up trying to figure himself out and forced himself to think about Thomas and who might have wanted to hurt him. Who would be willing or able to follow through on that desire. He laughed softly to himself. Everyone in this town seemed to have a rough edge. But being rough and being willing to hurt another human being were two completely different things.

To his right, Nico raised a hand slightly, as if waving a fly away from his paperwork. Adam turned his head, and out of the corner of his eye he saw a group of teenagers lingering outside the door of the *tabac*. One of the boys nodded and they all trouped around toward the side of the building.

"Ah, this is all I do now." Nico stood up straight and gestured toward his paperwork. "It is all about the government, here in France. The bureaucracy, you know?"

He looked at Adam, who simply shrugged. "Not really."

"Oh yes." Nico blew out a breath as he bent down to gather something from behind the bar. When he stood, he held two cartons of cigarettes. "It is very frustrating for a business owner, believe me. Forms for licenses, forms for taxes, now forms for grants ..." He rolled his eyes. "Do you need another coffee?"

Adam shook his head no.

"I'll be right back."

After Nico had left through the back door, Adam glanced at the papers Nico had been complaining about. It was clearly an application for something. Nico had suggested a grant, which made sense. Curious, Adam leaned closer to read more.

He could make out some of the application. It would be submitted to a nonprofit organization working with the French government and it seemed to be in support of opening new cafés in French villages. Adam let out a short laugh. That was a goal he could get behind.

As he sat back, a few words on the application caught his attention, and he leaned forward once more. Nico had written a sentence describing the current village café as *délabrée*. Adam recognized the French word for dilapidated and frowned. It was small, sure, and had limited hours, but that description seemed a stretch. Nor would he describe it as "*sur le point de fermer*," or "about to close" as Nico did in the very next sentence.

He heard Nico coming back into the room and slid back onto his stool. It wasn't really his business if Nico was stretching the truth on an application to the French government. On the other hand, being a cop was in his blood. It wasn't something Adam could let go of lightly.

He looked at Nico through different eyes as the bartender returned to his paperwork, stopping to add cash to the register on the way. The cartons of cigarettes were gone.

Adam looked outside but didn't see the group of teenagers passing by again. No doubt they had simply gone in a different direction. Adam might be new to France, but he recognized a black-market sale when he saw one.

So Nico was selling cigarettes to teenagers. And fudging the facts on a government form. Adam focused his eyes on his coffee as he thought this through. The man might be crooked, but that hardly made him a killer. Could small crimes lead a man to a bigger crime? To the biggest crime of all?

Adam had seen enough to know that they could. Either way, he would need to share a word to the wise with Julien before he left.

He looked at his watch. Enough daydreaming. It was time.

20

THE *MAIRIE* LOOKED DESERTED. Of course, Adam had yet to see it look busy, given the size of *Saint-Honoré*. But he was still surprised not to see any other client passing through the thick front door of the old stone building. Worn tiles paved the main entry hall, while three closed doors seemed designed to turn away any curious visitors. A wide, equally worn stone staircase led up to the second, or as they would say, first floor. Hearing voices coming from that level, Adam jogged up the steps.

He interrupted a fervent conversation at the top of the stairs, two women, both in gray skirts and sweaters, arguing forcefully. About what, he did not know. They stopped talking abruptly at his appearance.

One of the women shifted the pile of folders she was carrying to her left arm, using her now free right hand to pat down her hair and tuck a stray strand behind her ear. She smiled at Adam.

"*Bonjour*," she said.

"*Bonjour*," Adam replied with a smile, but his accent gave him away.

The second, slightly older woman asked how she could help. With some difficulty, Adam was able to communicate that he was looking for Chief Roche and learn that the object of his search could be found by exiting the building and walking around to the right, to a smaller entrance on the side. His offices, though technically within the *Mairie*, were not accessible from within.

Thanking them both, Adam retraced his steps, following the gravel path that led around the side of the building, past the parking lot and well-trimmed bushes. The glass door broke the monotony of the yellow stone, a small sign above the door proclaiming this to be the home of the *Police Municipale*.

Even before pulling the door open, Adam could see that the small room was empty. He entered nonetheless, thinking that if nothing else he could leave a note for Julien. It was actually his wife he was looking for anyway. The helpful secretary at her school had directed him here to find her in advance of their scheduled lunch date with the group of "descendants," as he had come to think of them. About which he was unusually nervous and hoping to gather advice and intelligence beforehand.

The anteroom of the police station held only a bench, a cork board covered in a variety of postings, and a small desk on a platform at the far end. The desk was unoccupied, but strewn about with papers, printed and handwritten. Adam approached the desk hoping to find a scrap of paper on which to leave a note, feeling a little surprised that the offices of the police would be left unattended, when he heard the voices.

A door leading off the waiting room stood ajar, and the voices were coming from beyond that doorway. Relieved that someone was, in fact, on duty at the station, Adam took a seat on the bench, planning to wait until he could knock on the door without interrupting. He'd only heard one voice, so he assumed whoever it was — and it sounded like Chief Roche — was on the phone and would finish soon enough.

A second voice made him realize his mistake. He recognized Margot's alto tones. Knowing he shouldn't, knowing he was invading both the personal space of a husband and wife and the professional space of the local Chief of Police, Adam listened. Or at least tried to. Both the Roche's spoke in clear, well-educated French, without the lilts of the local accent. That made it easier for him to understand, though he still only picked out about half of the words.

He shut his eyes, and let the words drift over him, knowing he would understand better if he didn't try to translate every word but instead listened for the meaning being conveyed.

Margot was offering words of consolation and support, that was clear. Julien had done the right thing, apparently.

Julien, on the other hand, was worried. He was limited — through ability or authority, Adam couldn't at first tell. Finally the words *police judiciare* jumped out at him. Of course. The local police in France were not authorized to investigate crimes, and certainly not crimes at the level of murder. The cork board facing him announced in bold letters that the mission of the *police municipale* was to support the functions and officers of the *police judiciare* and the *gendarmes*.

"*Mais Monsieur le Mairie est agreeable*," Margot said. The mayor agreed.

Agreed with what?

"This is ridiculous," Adam muttered as he stood. Why was he eavesdropping? He couldn't even understand what they were saying. Force of habit, he knew. He loved being a cop, but hated how it required him to pry into people's lives, their secrets, their hopes and fears.

His hand was on the door when he heard the words "*le crime de meurtre.*" Even in French, there was no mistaking the word murder.

He returned to his bench. So Thomas' death had been ruled a murder. It had taken long enough.

"... *Ça fait deux jours* ..." Julien was saying.

Exactly, already two days. It was conceivable that the local doctor had taken that long to draw a conclusion, though if any medical professional took two days to identify murder in Philly that doctor would be looking for a new job.

He listened again, focusing.

The doctor had confirmed murder last night ... had been concerned because these were his neighbors, his friends.

Of course, Adam could relate to that. No one wanted to suspect a friend of being a cold-blooded killer. This wouldn't have been good news to Julien. So he got the news last night, but hadn't yet called in the *gendarmes*. Was this what the mayor was supporting? Avoiding alerting the correct authorities?

Adam shook his head, no way.

But Margot repeated that the mayor trusted Julien and then she asked Julien why he didn't trust himself.

"I'm worried," Julien said. "I worry ... a murder ... in our town ... calling in the *police judiciare* right away."

Adam nodded, understanding clearly.

Then Margot spoke. "This is your chance," Adam heard distinctly. "You will catch a killer."

Adam stood and silently left the station.

21

THE CAFÉ in the square looked as peaceful as always. Bright Provençal sunlight left a patchwork of light and dark on the pavement between the awnings and trees, glinting off windows and wine glasses on outdoor tables. Three tables had been pushed together to accommodate a larger than usual group. Eight adults ranging in age from early forties to seventy years old gathered around it, chatting, laughing, shaking hands.

Adam felt a reluctance he'd never felt before. He could still leave. Run back to his hotel, pack his bags and never return. Never confront the truth about his own family, his ancestors and their acts.

He stepped forward out of the shadow of the grocers and into the open pavement around the café. Two of the adults saw him and nodded, gesturing for him to join them.

Adam looked around, hoping to find a familiar face, but saw none. He pulled out an empty chair and perched uncomfortably on an edge, waiting for someone else to start the conversation and wondering what language they would choose to talk in. To his great relief, Margot trotted in from a side street, waving as she ran.

"Adam, hello," she said, slightly out of breath. "I am sorry I am late." She stood at the head of the table and greeted all of the lunch guests. "*Mes amis, merci bien d'avoir participé.* Thank you so much for being here, my friends. Please, meet Adam Kaminski, from Philadelphia."

Adam's relief that she had switched to English was short-lived as he saw eight faces turn to stare at him.

"Um ... hello." Adam stood, feeling that was more appropriate to speak to the group at large. "I appreciate you taking the time to meet me, to talk to me about your families and their experiences. Perhaps Margot has told you, I am here because I am trying to find out what happened to my great-grandfather during the war."

"Was he a Jew?" A middle-aged man asked.

"Was he lost?" A woman added.

Adam shook his head. "No. Catholic. Polish. And he made it safely to America." He saw the lowered brows of confusion and plowed on. "I want to learn more about his time in Poland before he left, during the war. I have some letters ..." He looked around and knew he was saying too much. He was here to listen, not to talk.

He sat down. "Please, I would very much like to hear your stories."

A waiter appeared with carafes of rosé wine and some water. The lunch guests poured themselves wine, adding water to their taste, then each placed an order for their lunch. Not having seen a menu, Adam ordered a *croque monsieur*. It seemed likely the café would serve a classic French grilled ham and cheese sandwich.

As they ate and drank, the individuals gathered around the table took turns telling him their stories, the stories of their parents, their great-grandparents. They told stories of families and fortunes lost, homes confiscated, toys abandoned in terrified flight.

None of the people who had chosen to join them for lunch that day had fled Poland himself or herself.

"Monsieur Kanoza," a woman who had introduced herself as Madame Genay explained, "is the only one left." She looked to her right and grabbed the hand of the man sitting there. "Your father is the only one left to tell the story of what really happened, isn't he?"

"It is true," Monsieur Kanoza the younger nodded. "But we still talk, we keep the stories alive. We share what we know so that we — and others — will never forget."

"Both of your parents fled Poland, then?" Adam asked them. "Is everyone here a child of one of those who fled?"

"A child? No." Madame Genay gestured to a few middle-aged people at the other end of the tables. "Some are *petits enfants* — grandchildren, as you would say." The group looked up at her as she spoke about them. "But they carry on the stories and the traditions."

Madame Genay knew her friends. At first, they were reluctant to tell Adam the stories of their grandfather or grandmother, each of whom had escaped from Poland just as the Nazis were taking over, fleeing from the towns closest to the border, running north first, through Switzerland, then south, through strange countries, hiding in barns, in sheds, in woods. But as they spoke of small details, bits and pieces of the time, the stories eventually came out.

They were stories about previous generations, yet as Adam listened, it sounded as if each teller could remember the events himself or herself. The events, the dirt, the cold, the terror.

All told, over thirty children passed through *Saint-*

Honoré on their way west, escaping to the freedom of England or even America. Four remained in this town, adopted by locals. Each was young enough to acculturate quickly. Each was desperately wanted by the family that adopted them.

Adam watched this group of adults, the youngest in her early forties, talk about events from the 1930s and 1940s as if they were yesterday. The past was very much alive here in *Saint-Honoré*, at least among this group of people.

"Are there others who chose not to meet with me?" Adam asked Monsieur Kanoza as they sipped the last of the wine, taking the necessary time to digest their lunches.

"There are a few others," Monsieur Kanoza responded. "My father, we mentioned. He is old now, he rarely goes out."

"Sebastien Roux," Madame Genay added.

"Sebastien?" Adam leaned forward. "The young mechanic?"

"*Oui.*" Monsieur Kanoza nodded sadly. "He has troubles, I know. But how can we blame him, when we look at his past ... his family ... what they went through."

"Does that really justify his anger and violence now?" Adam asked, knowing his opinion leaked through his words.

Madame Genay raised an eyebrow. "Does it? I suppose that is a matter of opinion." She shrugged. "Not everyone who is angry is a descendant of one of the lucky children."

Adam smiled at her use of the word lucky, though compared to others they certainly were.

"How do you mean?"

"How ...?" Madame Genay asked.

"Sorry, I mean, who are you talking about?" Adam explained.

She looked at Monsieur Kanoza. These two shared a lot

of looks. Adam wondered what else they shared as they clasped hands once again. "Monsieur Bonnet." She finally answered.

"The historian. I've met him. He harbors resentment against the Vichy regime, certainly."

Monsieur Kanoza nodded. "They lost so much, that family."

"Not their lives," Madame Genay pointed out, "not their children."

Monsieur Kanoza dipped his head in recognition of her point. "No, not everything. But he is angry all the same. Remember the fight."

"Ach, that was years ago," Madame Genay laughed. "Who hasn't had such a youthful moment?"

"Hmm," Monsieur Kanoza wagged his head and dipped his lips into a frown, as if agreeing to disagree.

"Tell me," Adam asked, when it seemed like they were going to let the matter drop. "What fight?"

"The Dubois boy." Monsieur Kanoza grinned like a teenager. "Philippe put him in his place, oh yes."

"Dubois? I've heard that name." Adam said. "They supported the Vichy regime, right?"

"They did," Margot spoke over Adam's shoulder, joining the conversation. "But that was many years ago. Philippe was in a schoolyard fight with a boy from a family who didn't get along with his family. It means nothing."

Adam waited to see if anyone else would make the connection. When no one did, he spoke. "Thomas Lefebvre was from a family that supported the Vichy regime."

His words were greeted with silence and a few icy stares.

"There is no reason to speak badly of Thomas," Monsieur Kanoza said curtly.

Realizing his mistake, Adam apologized immediately, but the damage was done. The lunch was at an end.

As they gathered coats, scarves and purses, each said a friendly good-bye to the others. A group as united as any family could be, Adam supposed.

Before leaving, Monsieur Kanoza turned back to Adam. "You must never forget how important the past is, even today. Think about how bad the Vichy regime was, think what it means not to be able to trust your own government."

"It's hard to imagine, but I try," Adam explained.

Monsieur Kanoza nodded, satisfied with the answer. "Families like that of Thomas, who supported the Vichy regime, they suffered after the war ended when people turned against them. It is time for the suffering to end."

Adam was struck by the similarity to the sentiment express by Sebastien just that morning. He was also struck by a fact that he supposed he must have known all along: the past never stays in the past, and can most definitely be motive for murder.

22

Elise kept her eyes peeled for the dark green leaves of the winter savory she'd seen earlier this week. Savory would add the perfect touch to the meat she was slowly roasting for Adam's dinner. She knew it liked the sun on this side of town, covering the rocks on the dry banks of the river that marked the town's southeast border. In that, the herb had something in common with her. She paused in her quest to once again appreciate her surroundings.

A shadow passed overhead and she looked up to see a bird of prey circling. The water was low, unusually so for October, so perhaps he had his eyes on the fish swimming just below the surface. Beautiful, but dangerous.

She resumed her search and found the savory with ease, cutting off a few branches, just enough for her meal that evening. She would come back for more whenever she needed it. It comforted her to know that everything she needed was right here, somewhere in *Saint-Honoré*. Another shadow passed overhead and she frowned, her mind turning to Andrew and the problems he might now be facing.

Why was he spending so much time with Sebastien, she wondered. Young men, similar ages, of course they would become friends. But that man was no good, even Elise could see that. Andrew needed good influences, not bad. He'd had enough of those in the past.

Pushing aside her worries, she ambled back down the river bank, a round-about way back to the main square, the café and their apartment. A mound of blue fabric caught her eye, an unnatural pile of rags in this otherwise pristine countryside. Irritated, she walked over, intending to pick it up and throw it away.

As she got closer, it moaned and rolled over.

"Enzo!" Elise recognized the old man as soon as he moved. "Enzo, what happened?" She ran to him and kneeled at his side, afraid to touch him but afraid not to. Finally, she put a hand gently on his arm, then on his face, to see if he was conscious.

He was, but disoriented. He mumbled a few incoherent words, then rolled over and spit out blood. More blood had seeped through one of his trouser legs and his hands were scraped and bloodied.

She stood frantically, scanning the area for movement. Someone was walking on the road coming out of town, too far away to recognize.

"Help! Help!" She called out as she ran toward the figure. It heard her and picked up speed, narrowing the distance.

As she recognized Nico, she called again, "Oh, Nico, help. It's Enzo, he's been hurt."

By now, the two had reached each other. Nico put two strong hands on her arms, holding her at a distance but offering comfort in his strength and his calm. The satchel looped over his shoulder sagged as he grabbed her, the top of a bottle of wine poking out. He pushed it back behind him as he said, "Where, show me."

She grabbed his hand and pulled him back to the river, to Enzo's still and beaten form.

"Ah, Enzo, Enzo, what have you done now?" Nico muttered as he rolled the old man over, prodding his arms, legs, chest.

"Is he okay?" Elise asked.

"Okay?" Nico looked up at her skeptically. "He's been badly beaten. No, I would not say he is okay. Enzo," he turned to the old man. "Can you hear me?"

Enzo grunted and nodded. Elise let her breath go and realized she'd been holding it. "He's alive."

Nico flinched and looked up at her. "I am so sorry. I forgot that you found Thomas. This must have been a terrible shock for you."

Elise nodded, but pointed at Enzo. "What can we do? He must go to a doctor."

"No," Enzo spoke for the first time, using his favorite word. "No. Leave me alone."

He tried to push Nico away, but he was too weak to be effective.

"Enzo, you are hurt. Who did this to you? What happened?" Nico asked.

"Mind your own business," Enzo grunted, his words blurred but now comprehensible.

Nico stood, wiping his hands on his pants.

"We can't just leave him here," Elise said, shocked.

"Don't be ridiculous, of course not." Nico's anger surprised her and she took a step back. "But what can we do? We can't drag him to see a doctor."

"Bring him to my house." Elise had no idea why she'd

said it, but she did. "I will wash him up, feed him, help him feel better. Maybe then he will see a doctor."

Nico knelt down before the old man. "Enzo, will you come to Elise's? She can offer you a warm meal, perhaps a bath?"

Enzo rolled over onto his side, his back to them, and Elise worried how they would manage if he said no. Could they carry him? Nico was a strong man, no doubt, but Enzo was a big man, too.

Enzo rolled back over, grabbed Nico's arm and pulled himself up into a sitting position. He spat again, this time with less blood.

"Come on," Nico grunted as he stood the old man up. "Can you walk?"

Enzo took a tentative step and stumbled.

"Hold on to me." Nico draped Enzo's arm over his shoulder, wrapping his own arm around Enzo's waist. "Elise, you may need to help as well."

Elise wrapped her arm around Enzo from the other side and held tight as they made their way, step by step, back to the town.

23

TODAY, the front door opened immediately at his knock. Monsieur Bonnet muttered something that may have been a greeting and ushered Adam into his home.

The inside of the house looked exactly as the outside did: cluttered, messy and worn. Thick, lavish curtains that hadn't been dusted in years blocked most of the light that would otherwise have exposed the front rooms to the bright afternoon sun. In the dimness, Adam could see heavy oak furniture, still strong but scarred with age. A cluster of glass ornaments and vases stood on one bookshelf, some chipped, all coated in a layer of dust. But most of all, Adam saw books. Lots and lots of books. They were piled up on almost all available surfaces, spilling off chairs and benches onto the floor, stacked layers deep on shelves, even balanced on the arms of the sofa and chairs.

Philippe kept moving through the front rooms and Adam followed him to a large, airy kitchen at the back of the house. Perhaps because it received less direct sunlight, no heavy curtains hung here, which gave the room a much friendlier atmosphere. At Philippe's direction, Adam took a seat at an ornately carved table, looking out onto the back-yard and garage he had seen on his first visit.

Philippe bustled about, preparing two espressos and bringing them over to the table with a plate of small biscuits. Adam thanked him and took a sip. Philippe downed his in one gulp and placed the empty cup back in its saucer.

"Now, tell me more," the old man said.

So Adam did. He started from the beginning — at least, what was the beginning for him. He knew his great-grandfa-ther, Witold Kaminski, had left Poland during the war, but he'd first learned there had been something mysterious about the flight from his cousin in Warsaw. From that first clue, Adam had followed the trail that led him here, to this tiny French town, in possession of photocopies of coded letters that had been archived at the Bermuda Station Hotel, a censorship station during the war and now the home to one of the best archives of World War II written materials available.

Philippe couldn't hide his excitement as he glanced over the copies Adam handed him. "Your great-grandfather, Witold Kaminski, exchanged these letters with a teacher here in *Saint-Honoré*, a man calling himself Faure?" Philippe spoke aloud, but Adam could tell he was simply thinking through the process. "This is clearly a code — look here." He jabbed at the paper with a thick finger. "No one would write this way. 'A chirpy dog,'" he quoted from the letter, translating as he read. "That means nothing, that is unintelligible. But to someone who understands ..." his words drifted off, and he kept reading.

Eventually, he glanced up at Adam. "Witold Kaminski spoke French?"

Adam shrugged. "I can only assume, I didn't know him. But his son did, my grandfather, so perhaps."

Bonnet nodded. "It was not uncommon in Poland, and other countries as well. French was the language of the arts, of diplomacy, of life."

Adam thought wryly that English had long since taken over as the world's *lingua franca*, but kept the thought to himself.

Finally, Bonnet dropped the papers onto the table. "I will see what I can find out about our so-called Monsieur Faure. I do not know the name. But if he was involved in the resistance, he would not be using his true identity."

Adam flinched a little but tried to keep his expression clear. He sincerely hoped that the mysterious Faure was, in fact, involved in the resistance, or he would soon be found to be a liar.

Bonnet continued, "I will go through my records, old letters, notes, newspapers. But you must understand — " he wagged a finger at Adam "— most was not written down. This was dangerous work. But I will see what I can piece together."

Adam left Monsieur Bonnet digging through a pile of books in one of the front rooms, feeling more optimistic about his quest than he had in quite a while. The afternoon sun was full and he turned his face up to it, to enjoy the warmth even as the wind picked up, reminding him that it was already October.

He had plans to meet with Elise for dinner, to talk about how he could help her and Andrew in any way. He hadn't done much for her yet, and felt guilty. Here she was offering him free meal after meal, and the most he'd offered so far was a true appreciation of her cooking.

His walk from Bonnet's, on the outskirts of town, to the café took him past the *Mairie*. Five black vehicles crammed into the paved space in front of the town hall, each marked with the logo of the Gendarmerie. So Julien had called them in. Adam was glad to know they were investigating, though he couldn't imagine how it would feel to have to hand any investigation over to the national force instead of investigating locally.

Arriving at the café, he pushed the door open and called out. A voice responded from the kitchen, but when he stuck his head in, he saw only the chef, Henri, busy prepping food at a long counter. When asked, Henri directed Adam to an unmarked door at the back of the kitchen.

Adam took the narrow wooden stairs up one level to a store room for the café — bags of flour, sacks of potatoes and onions along one wall, fresh cutlery, napkins and dishes behind glass shelving on the other. One more flight of stairs led him to another unmarked door. He knocked.

"Adam, please come in."

Adam hid his surprise to be greeted by Nico in Elise' apartment. "What's going on?"

"Elise is in the bedroom with Enzo, he's been hurt."

"What? How?" Adam felt his anger rise. Enzo may have been rude, but he had a spark of life and humor in him that Adam appreciated.

"Elise is with him." Nico put a hand on Adam's shoulder. "We must wait."

Adam paced around the small living room, barely taking in the few pieces of furniture, worn but clean, a watercolor of a local scene hanging on the wall near a window that looked out onto the town square.

The door to what must have been the bedroom swung open, and Enzo pushed his way into the room, using one hand to fend Elise off.

"Get off of me. I do not need your help." His voice was as grizzled as his face. "Let me be."

Nico laughed. "Looks like he's feeling better."

Elise shook her head even as she nodded a greeting to Adam. "He had a few cuts and bruises that I tried to bandage. The cut on his leg is quite serious and I told him he needs to see a doctor."

"Pah," Enzo responded. He noticed Adam at that point. "You brought over the American to make fun of the poor old man?"

"No Enzo, of course not." Nico stepped forward, a hand out. "We want to help you. We do not think less of you for being attacked."

"Pah." Enzo waved his hand away and turned his back to Adam. "I can take care of myself."

"Have you contacted Margot?" Adam asked Elise under his breath. "She will want to know about this."

"We did," Elise nodded. "As soon as we got back here. She will meet him at his cottage."

"Then hopefully she will convince him to have his wounds cared for," Nico added. In a louder voice, he said, "Come, Enzo, I will walk you home."

He tried to put an arm around the old man's shoulders, but he batted him away. Nico rolled his eyes, then gestured for Enzo to go first. As Enzo left, Nico turned back to Adam and Elise, both standing by the window. "This is not good, you know. Two people have been beaten in our town."

"Two? Are Enzo's injuries similar to Thomas'?" Adam asked. "I haven't heard any details."

Elise shuddered and wrapped her arms around herself. "They are similar, yes. Thomas had an injury to his head, as if he'd been struck. That could have happened to Enzo." Her voice faltered and she looked down.

Nico nodded to Adam and followed Enzo out of the room.

Adam wrapped one arm around Elise and guided her to a chair, then followed the smell of roasting meat down a hallway to her kitchen to fetch her a glass of water. Something stronger might be better, but he figured this was a start. When he got back to the living room, he found her once again standing by the window.

"Here, drink this."

She accepted with thanks and took a sip. "I don't know where Andrew is," she whispered.

"Andrew? Are you worried he's been hurt as well?"

She shook her head. "No, I worry ..." She stopped talking and looked up at Adam as if suddenly recognizing him. She shook away whatever she'd been thinking. "I am sorry. It's nothing. No, I have no reason to worry about Andrew. Now, I have a meal cooking for you, I only have to add a few more herbs. We can eat in an hour, sound good?"

"Works for me." Adam nodded, recognizing her need to change the topic of conversation.

"And perhaps an aperitif while we wait?" she asked, opening a low cabinet stocked with a variety of bottles.

"Even better," Adam said. But he couldn't ignore the fact that Nico had a point. This couldn't be a coincidence. "We have to consider there might be a connection."

"What do you mean?" Elise's voice was sharp and she paused, bottle held in the air above two glasses.

"Nico is right, two people have been attacked. What are the chances it's not connected?"

Elise let out a deep breath and sank onto a chair, both of her hands wrapped around the tiny aperitif glass. Adam picked up his and sat next to her, close, their legs touching.

"How do we find out?" she asked.

Adam shook his head. "We try to learn more. More about Thomas and about Enzo — who would want to hurt them? Who did they anger, for example. Or who benefits from their deaths?"

Elise looked at Adam, her eyes wide. "No one benefits."

Adam shrugged and took a drink.

After thinking for a moment, Elise said, "I can show you more about Thomas. Perhaps if you understand him the way I do, you'll have a better chance of figuring this out."

"Sure. What can you show me?"

Elise stood and walked down the hall to the kitchen, talking over her shoulder as she walked. "We can go to his house. His farmhouse. You can learn about him there."

"Oh no," Adam's response was firm. "No way. That'll still be a crime scene. We can't break in."

"We don't have to break in," Elise pleaded, coming back into the sitting room. "I can get in, no problem. No breaking and entering." Seeing the refusal in Adam's eyes, she continued. "I have to know it wasn't Andrew. Don't you see?"

"Don't you already know?" Adam asked, wondering not for the first time how much Elise really thought Andrew might have done this terrible deed.

"Yes, of course, I meant to say that we have to find out who really killed Thomas so that Andrew isn't suspected. You will you help me, as you agreed?" She sat next to Adam and grabbed his hands in hers. "Please."

Adam took a breath but couldn't pull his eyes away from hers, dark and pleading. He shook his head at his own stupidity, knowing he was going somewhere he shouldn't. "I suppose the police will have already searched it. So it wouldn't hurt. Though —" he pulled his hands free and held up a finger to stop her from thanking him, "— since the police did already search it, it's not like we're going to find any clues or anything. We can just look around so I can learn more about Thomas."

Elise grinned widely and nodded. "Thank you. Thank you. And besides, you never know what we'll find. The police didn't know about this second attack when they were searching."

"No, that's true ..." Adam considered this. "And if Enzo refuses to report it, they still won't. Well then, we'll tell Julien."

"And then go to Thomas's house?" Elise asked eagerly.

"We're not breaking in, right?"

"Of course not, Thomas was like family to me. I know how to get into his house. We don't need to break in."

She jumped up to see to the meal. Adam could see the excitement in her gait. He had been the one to raise the point that he needed to learn more about Thomas, but seeing how excited Elise was about visiting Thomas' farm, Adam had to wonder, what exactly was she looking for? Proof that Andrew didn't do it because someone else did? Or clues that could implicate him to get rid of?

24

"THIS IS A BAD IDEA." Adam kept his eyes on the ground as he spoke to avoid twisting an ankle in one of the many dips and holes that pitted the orchard.

Elise stopped and stared at him, hands on her hips. "Last night you said you would help me."

"I know, and I will." Adam held up a hand to calm her down. "I can't tell you how much I appreciate the way you got Mr. Bonnet to change tunes and agree to help me. But this ..."

He gazed around them. Gnarled trunks of ancient gray trees stood in uneven rows, denuded of their fruit. The olives had been harvested just the week before, and the trees looked almost lonely, waiting for their next chance to blossom.

"We aren't even on Thomas' land yet," Elise said, the strain she felt coming out in the tightness of her voice. "And I told you, I go to his home all the time. I know how to get in. I'm always welcome there. We're not breaking in."

"Maybe not breaking, but definitely entering," Adam muttered, but continued following Elise.

Their decision to look over Thomas' house to see if they could find anything useful had seemed reasonable last night as they developed the plan. It seemed a lot less reasonable in the light of day. Or maybe he just hadn't thought she'd really want to go through with it. True, Enzo refused to admit what had happened to him. He insisted he had simply tripped and fallen, even after the doctor who stitched him up pointed out that his wounds were inconsistent with a fall and much more consistent with being hit by a blunt object.

Adam was just glad Margot had convinced him to get medical help.

But as long as Enzo refused to talk, the police would never connect an old man's injuries with the death of Thomas Lefebvre.

Julien had been a little understanding that morning when Elise and Adam tried to report Enzo's attack. But not much.

"You understand that I am not investigating this case, do you not?" Julien replied with frustration. Adam could only imagine what it was like for him.

"Can't you at least investigate Enzo's attack?" he asked.

Julien shook his head. "*Non*. That would also be a matter for the *gendarmes*, and at the moment they are far more interested in the murder investigation. Now, if Enzo comes forward to say he was attacked, they might agree the two incidents are connected ..." He ended on a raised, questioning tone, but Adam and Elise both shook their heads.

"He will not."

"No way."

"So, there we are." Julien shrugged.

"What if you tell the *gendarmes* about the attack?" Elise asked.

"Hmph," Julien sniffed. "They are not interested in my help, except as I can direct traffic in town so they avoid any delays."

Adam grinned. "I know the type, believe me."

"No, no." Julien waved his hands. "I regret saying that. We have a very good system of policing here. I am proud to play my part in it. This investigation is simply beyond my responsibilities." He lowered his eyes as he continued. "I must do my job. You understand"

Adam did understand. While he'd always been willing to follow an investigation wherever it took him, his partner Pete worked strictly by the book. And Adam respected him all the more for it.

"You're a good cop," Adam told Julian as he shook his hand. "Before we go, is there anything else you can tell us about Thomas' death. Anything that we wouldn't have heard already?"

Julien laughed out loud at this. "What makes you think I would tell you, even if there was?" He looked at them both, the accusation clear in his eyes. "Whatever you are planning, be very careful. Do not put yourselves on the wrong side of the law."

Adam bit his tongue but couldn't avoid looking at Elise. "Absolutely," he said. "No breaking the law, right Elise?"

She smiled and nodded. "Of course not." A picture of innocence.

Right. "But I hope you understand," he said to Julien, "we may be back."

Half an hour later, Adam and Elise were approaching Thomas' farmhouse from the back. Adam looked over at Elise. "You know as well as I do that we're hampering a murder investigation if we go in there. If the *gendarmes* don't want Julien's help, you can be damn sure they don't want mine or yours either."

"Which is why I didn't tell Julien where we were going." Elise shrugged. "And we're not hindering any investigation, we are simply visiting the home of a dead friend."

"A friend your brother may be suspected of killing," Adam pointed out.

"A friend who has invited me over so many times. See?" Elise led them to a pair of large windows on the back of the farmhouse, their frames peeling and brown.

Adam saw no police guard, no caution tape. Perhaps the *gendarmes* had come and gone and it was no longer a crime scene, he told himself. He didn't believe himself.

She grabbed a frame with both hands, planting her feet in the fresh earth of the garden to steady herself. With a quick jerk, the window opened, its scraping sound disturbing a flock of birds in the orchard. Elise grinned triumphantly. "This window is always open, so that Andrew and I would have a way in."

She slipped in through the narrow opening. Once inside, she pushed it open farther to admit Adam, waving him in when he didn't move right away.

Elise was acting like a woman obsessed. Finding Enzo seemed to have been the final straw for her. Her concern about Andrew, her worries that he would be implicated in the attack or the murder, drove her to act irrationally. Adam shouldn't be supporting that.

On the other hand, he had agreed to help her in exchange for her help with his quest, and she'd done what she promised. There was no good reason for them to search Thomas' house, he knew that. Surely, the *gendarmes* had already searched it thoroughly. But they hadn't known about the second attack — that could change what they were looking for.

Plus, if it made Elise feel like she was doing something, that was a good thing in itself. And if they did find anything that gave them a clue as to who had killed Thomas, they would immediately turn that over to Julien. What the hell, the new Chief of Police in Philadelphia was known to treat the rules as flexible, why shouldn't he?

He stepped in through the open window.

25

ADAM STRAIGHTENED up at the sound of a tractor passing by on the street. He'd been squatting in front of a bookcase, reading the spines without touching anything. He'd done his best over the past hour not to touch anything, acutely aware of the need to leave as little evidence of their search as possible. The sound of the tractor moved away and Adam let out the breath he'd been holding.

Elise didn't seem to have the same concern. She flipped over pillows on sofas and chairs, pulled books off of shelves, even dug through the kitchen cabinets.

Thomas Lefebvre's house was an old family farmstead, with generations of Lefebvres posing in pictures that covered walls and surfaces in the home.

Siblings, cousins, children, laughing and smiling. Parents and grandparents. Then older pictures, beautiful sepia-toned prints, with unsmiling French men and women. The earliest photos seemed to be from the century before last, before the violent upheavals of the twentieth century. Women in long skirts looked sternly at the camera, men with farm tools adopted bold poses.

"These are his ancestors, right?" Adam asked as Elise paused beside him.

"They are. I understand from Thomas that they worked on a farm not far from here, just two towns over."

"They were farm laborers?"

Elise nodded. "Something like that, yes."

"He's come a long way, then. Now he owns the farm and hires others."

Elise shrugged. "It happens. I believe in his family's case their fortunes improved dramatically during the war."

"Because they supported the regime?" Adam asked.

"Perhaps. And because others didn't, and those people lost what little they had."

Adam shook his head as he continued his search.

In the kitchen, he saw only a few dishes, the most basic of cookware. "Thomas not much of a cook?"

Elise laughed under her breath. "Definitely not. He relied on the generosity of the village women."

"They took care of him?"

"Hm." Elise wagged her head. "So to speak. Every now and then someone would stop by with a dish for him, something she'd made special that week, maybe she had leftovers."

Adam considered this. The local women taking care of the town's bachelor? Or was this something more? "Was there much competition over Thomas?" he asked.

"Over?" Elise shook her head in confusion.

"For his affections. You know, it's a small town, a small eligible male population."

Elise laughed out loud. "Definitely not, no." She laughed again. "Thomas was not that kind of man. Plus there was that family history ..." her voice trailed off.

"Camille liked him well enough," Adam pointed out.

"That's true ..." Elise let her eyes roam over the kitchen. "She has ... unusual tastes in men though."

Adam followed Elise's gaze. Two cups stood drying in the rack next to the sink.

"Two cups?" Adam asked, stepping forward to look at them without touching, though they'd clearly been washed.

"Makes sense. Andrew was here early. Thomas would have offered him coffee."

Adam looked around the kitchen once more then stepped out to the main hall. He didn't know what he was looking for, not really. Anything obvious would have been found by the police, any evidence of a burglary would have been identified. But he'd dug through victim's homes enough times in the past to know that sometimes the clues that pointed to a killer were not so easy to recognize. If nothing else, he could find clues that would help fill in the blanks for him about Thomas himself — his likes, his loves. Sometimes the best way to find a killer was to understand the victim.

He stared at a beautifully framed print of Thomas standing with his arm wrapped around a slightly younger Camille. "He didn't have children?" he asked.

"I suppose he was waiting for the right time. He has two sisters, they both live in Paris. I'm sure they're on their way. They will be his main heirs." Elise picked up a pile of printed photographs as she answered, flipping through them.

"Did Thomas have a will?" Adam asked her.

Elise shrugged. "Perhaps. Without children, he had the option to leave parts of his estate to others of his choosing. But the bulk will go to his nearest French relative."

"Option?" Adam asked, surprised.

"Oh yes." Elise smiled. "French law. Everything a

person owns always goes to the children. No exceptions. Well, this is interesting."

She held up one of the prints for Adam to look at. It was a photograph of a man and a woman kissing. The shot had been taken from a distance, with a few trees and passing people blocking the view but the kissing couple nevertheless visible.

"Why is that interesting?"

Elise wiggled her eyebrows. "Because that—" she pointed at the man in the picture "— is Eduoard Berger. And that—" here she indicated the woman "— is not his wife."

Adam rolled his eyes as he shook his head. "Small towns. I just don't get it. So, you're saying Thomas didn't have kids."

"Right." Elise dropped the prints back onto the shelf. "So ... for example, he might have had an arrangement with Nico that he would inherit the winery."

"Nico certainly seems to think so." Adam responded.

"Oh yes?" Elise asked, interested. "Did he say so?"

Adam nodded, turning his attention to another photo. This one showed a young Margot with a woman who bore a striking resemblance to Thomas. "Is this one of his sisters?" he asked.

"They were in school together. The sister left for Paris, Thomas stayed here. Thomas is a little older. He took over the family farm after their parents died."

"I didn't realize Margot knew his family that well."

"This is a small town, Adam. Everyone knows everyone that well."

"Hm." Adam laughed under his breath. "So why did the rest of the family leave?"

Elise lifted one shoulder, her face a picture of dismissal.

"The ridiculous stories. You know, you've heard them. They left to get away from the stigma of their family's history."

Adam paused, watching her. "So why did Thomas stay?"

Elise shook her head. "Thomas really didn't care what other people thought."

"Good to know." He moved to the far side of the room, his eyes running over a shelf of neatly stacked logbooks. "Are these business records?"

Elise pulled one down and leafed through it. "Yes, for the lavender farm." She replaced it and picked up a different colored book. "This seems to be a personal diary. And this one is for the winery. All very neat and organized. He ran an organized business." She frowned as she flipped through the pages of one book. "Hmmm. These logs show that he was losing money on the lavender farm. I'm surprised. It's very popular in this area."

"I guess it makes sense then that he's branching out to wine," Adam said. His eyebrows lowered, and he looked away from Elise as he added in a low voice, "But it also means Andrew's job could be in jeopardy."

"Nonsense," Elise retorted. "Andrew could simply work on the vineyard instead, that's all."

"What does this say?" Adam asked, pulling on a piece of paper taped to the front of one logbook. It came off in his hands and he handed it to Elise.

"It says, '*C'est n'importe quoi.*'" She read aloud, then glanced up at him. "That's nonsense, ridiculous."

"Why is it ridiculous? What does it mean?"

"No," she laughed. "That's what it means. That's what this note says."

"And it's stuck to the front of the winery business logs? That can't be normal."

"No ..." Elise flipped through the rest of the pages of the log, then pulled out another. "He has logs for each year that he's been growing the grapes. He's selling them to a *négociant*, this shows the income he's made each year."

Adam glanced at it. "That's not bad."

"No? That's just the income, this shows his expenses. His profits are surprisingly low, frankly."

Adam looked again. "Well, he was just starting out in the wine business, right?"

"I suppose ..."

"You don't sound convinced."

"Let's take these." She looked up at Adam. "I can ask Nico to help explain them to me."

"Elise, it's bad enough I let you talk me into breaking in here. We can't walk away with his property."

She bit her lip and looked at him and Adam could read the mental battle in her eyes.

"What are you really looking for, Elise? Why are we here?" He waved his hand at the logbooks. "Did we come here to steal business records?"

"Of course not," Elise's voice rose. "I was looking ... I don't know. Something. But it doesn't matter, there's nothing."

"Then leave the books, Elise. They're not ours." Adam put a gentle hand on her arm but she shook it off.

"But don't they belong to Nico now? After all, the winery is his, isn't it?"

"Not until the courts say it is."

A voice carried through the room, someone calling from the vineyard. Adam couldn't tell how close. "Look, we gotta go. We've been here long enough."

He headed back toward the windows through which

they'd entered, but turned when he realized Elise wasn't following him.

She stood in the living room, her eyes scanning the rows of figures in the books.

"Are you coming?"

She didn't respond.

"Fine, suit yourself." He left her standing in the living room, flipping through logbooks.

26

Elise found Nico standing just outside the back door of his *tabac*, hands on hips, staring at the grass.

"Nico?" She finally spoke when it was clear he hadn't noticed her coming through the *tabac*.

"Elise. *Bonjour*." He leaned down to kiss her cheeks. "How is Enzo? Have you heard from Margot?"

"Yes, he is doing well I understand. Thank you, again, for your help yesterday. I don't know what I would have done if you hadn't been passing."

Nico put a hand on her shoulder. "I am glad I was there, as well."

She followed his gaze over the open yard that filled the space behind the *tabac*, stretching from the end of the drive from which a car peeked out to the stone wall of the neighboring property. It looked like he'd been doing some work in the yard — a pile of concrete blocks stood in one corner, a toolbox resting next to them. And Andrew's gloves lying on top of the toolbox. She let out a breath of relief as she smiled. "What are you looking at, Nico?"

"The future. Do you see it?" he grinned broadly. "I have

some ideas for using this space, you see. To expand the *tabac*, perhaps to add a restaurant."

Elise raised an eyebrow. "We already have several cafés, including mine. Do you really think we have the need for another restaurant?"

"Perhaps not yet," Nico shrugged. "But I have plans for this town, too. We must grow, Elise, don't you see? We must bring in more visitors, more tourists. Like Monsieur Kaminski, who I see you've been spending time with?" He lifted his voice into a gentle question.

Elise felt herself blush, but ignored the implications. "Yes, I see what you're saying. Well, if you have ways to get more people to visit our little town, I'll support you in that. But that's not why I'm here." She lifted three logbooks out of the shopping bag she carried. "I need your help understanding these."

Nico's eyes widened as he recognized what Elise held. "You have Thomas' logs? For the winery?" He smiled broadly. "Thank you! I have been asking Julien when I can get access to these, but I was told I had to wait."

Elise cleared her throat uncomfortably. "Well, yes, the thing is... they don't actually know I have them."

Nico grinned again. "Elise, I had no idea you were so sneaky."

"Look," Elise explained as she followed Nico to a table at the back of the *tabac*. The regular customers clustered around the bar at the front, and Nico shot them a glance to make sure they were all happily drinking. "Thomas had so many logs. He kept notes about everything, it seems, from the farm to the vineyard to his personal accounts. It took a while going through his diaries, but I found these logs specifically about the vineyard, and I don't understand this note." She handed Nico the note, then slid one of the books open. "It looks like he was not doing as well as he could have been. Oh." She stopped when she saw Nico's annoyance. "I'm sorry. Of course, this was your business as well, wasn't it?"

"It *is* my business," Nico said sharply. "And I agree, we were not doing as well as we could have been. But I have plans to change that." He pulled the logs toward him and started flipping through them.

She waited as he perused the books, even as he got up twice to serve his patrons. After ten minutes of waiting, he spoke again. "We have been selling the grapes to a *négociant*, because it's the easiest and fastest way to make a profit on a new winery. But I will consider now creating our own wine, a new label."

"Are you able to do that? I mean, have you tried it yet?"

"In fact, we have not had that opportunity." Nico spoke sadly. "Thomas had some ideas along these lines, but wasn't willing to do anything about it. Now I will follow up on his ideas, and I know it will be a great wine. I have barrels—" he cut himself off. "Well, anyway, yes I will make some changes. I hope to improve this. Is that what you wanted to know?" he asked curiously.

"About that note?" Elise prompted him.

"Ah, that." He looked at it again. "No, I don't know what that is about. Perhaps it's not about these logs at all? You said he had others?" His gaze sharpened. "What other logs did you find?"

Elise frowned and blew out a breath. "As I said, all kinds of diaries. I suppose this could have been meant for another one and when it fell, he simply stuck it to the front of this. But he was so careful, that doesn't sound like him." She looked up at Nico, confused. "And I'm surprised that

Thomas wouldn't follow through if he had ideas for making a good wine."

"A great wine." Nico interrupted her with a smile.

"Yes," Elise's frown didn't fade. "I always thought Thomas was the sort of person who made things work. If he had dreams, he would follow them. Even if it meant taking a loss for a year or two, he was always investing in his future."

Nico stood, tossing his towel over his shoulder. "Well, I can't help you there. I know he was eager to continue selling the grapes to the *négociant*. Look, I have to go. It is lunchtime soon and I will be getting busier."

"Right, sure." Elise stood. "I need to open the café. Thank you for your help, Nico."

"Of course." His reply was curt as he turned back to his business. She watched his back for a moment, wondering how she and Nico could have such different impressions of the same man.

27

SEBASTIEN LIVED toward the eastern edge of the small town, alone in the house he'd grown up in. His father had been a local artist, Adam had learned from Elise, selling paintings of the countryside and nearby chateaux. He'd done well enough to support his family and even allow for a relatively comfortable retirement. Both parents had chosen to move to Paris to live near their other children. A common occurrence, he was beginning to understand, as small towns like this slowly died off due to lack of opportunities and a dearth of young people willing to help them grow. It wasn't a large house and it had certainly seen better days, but Adam found himself surprised by how neat and well-tended the front yard looked.

Flower boxes at the front windows overflowed with bright red and white geraniums, while the door and window trim looked like they had recently been painted a festive green. The gray stone structure was three levels high, the top level looking like an attic, with only a lone, small dormer window opening onto the street.

Following his natural curiosity, Adam took the stone

path that led around to the back. As he turned off the main road, he saw Nico in the distance, coming toward him. He stepped rapidly behind the house. Last thing he needed was for someone to see him. Though even as he moved quickly away, he wondered why Nico was walking toward the *tabac* from the direction of Thomas' farm. He should've been busy in the *tabac* at this time of day.

Sebastien's house, though more than adequate for one man living alone, was dwarfed by the giant barn behind it. Not yet sure how he could best approach Sebastien, Adam followed the stone path that took him to the barn, then walked around it, considering his options.

He had agreed to help Elise, after all. Monsieur Bonnet was working on his own research, Adam had nothing else to do while waiting. It was time to talk to the suspects, and the first person Adam suspected was Sebastien Roux.

This would not be a friendly chat. Not after their encounter at the *tabac* the other day. He needed more leverage. He needed to know more about Sebastien — more than that he was a young man with a violent temper and a grudge against the man he thought his girlfriend was still in love with.

A few texts with Pete had made it clear that he wasn't going to get any help from his contacts in the PPD. More than that, he had to keep a very low profile while in France. Apparently Captain Hillyard was only willing to stretch the limits of the rules when it benefitted him personally. Or so Pete implied — it was too risky to put something that direct into a text message.

The barn door was propped ajar, not quite enough for Adam to see inside. And he wasn't about to commit another illegal act today. One per day was probably enough, he laughed to himself under his breath. Walking around the far side, he saw that the wall on this side of the barn had been fitted with a row of large mullioned windows. The work must have been done years ago — the glass was cracked in a few places and dirt accumulated in the corners and between the individual panes. But he could see through clearly, which was exactly what he needed.

Within, the barn was as neat and orderly as the front of the house. Rather than the art supplies he supposed this workspace had been designed for, the barn now served as a mechanics workshop. A series of wall panels held Sebastien's trade equipment — wrenches, pliers, calipers all cleaned and neatly stored. A work surface stood just in front of the windows through which Adam looked, set up, he imagined, to make best use of the light the windows allowed in.

Adam let his eyes roam over the equipment, the work surface, the benches on the far side of the room, the shelves stacked with rags and gloves, overalls and jackets that hung from pegs. Once again, he realized he'd been expecting a mess, a disorganization that matched his understanding of Sebastien's personality. But he knew from long experience that people could compartmentalize. While Sebastien might be angry and chaotic in his personal life, he clearly kept his professional life neat and methodical.

He had to admit, he was almost impressed. Almost. That rage he'd witnessed still spoke of a man who didn't have complete control over his emotions.

Adam's thoughts focused as his eyes fell on a piece of blackened metal. It stuck out from under a piece of clothing that looked like it had fallen from one of the pegs on the wall. That, alone, had caught Adam's attention, since it was out of place in this well-organized space. But the metal said even more.

Adam recognized it, he thought. It was the same engine part he'd seen Sebastien carrying two days ago, when he'd followed him to the repair shop. He must simply have picked it up again, Adam chided himself. This wasn't a clue.

But if he'd simply picked up a part that had been repaired, why leave it lying on the floor? Why not put it back where it belonged? And more importantly, what was stuck to it? For he could clearly see some greenery stuck to the pipe. Grass, perhaps, or weeds. They adhered to the pipe through a dark substance that must have been sticky. Could be dirt, Adam knew. But it could also be blood.

28

ADAM PULLED open the glass door of the police station for the second time that day. This time, he wasn't going to take no for an answer. He'd definitely seen something worth investigating in Sebastien's barn.

Instead of Julien, Margot Roche stood in the little waiting room, staring at the cork board. "Monsieur Kaminski, how nice to see you." She came towards him and kissed his cheeks. He still hadn't figured out that particular routine, and tried awkwardly to return the kisses.

"I'm looking for your husband," he said. "Is he here?"

"He is, but I'm afraid you'll have to wait. As do I." She gestured toward the bench. "I am glad to have this chance to talk with you, however. We haven't spoken since our lunch yesterday."

Adam nodded as he lowered himself onto the bench. Margot settled down next to him and turned to face him, uncomfortably close for him, but she didn't seem to notice.

"Thank you so much for arranging that. I learned a lot, to be sure," he told her. "I still don't know what role my own ancestors played in that tragedy, but it was eye opening to hear those stories."

"I thought it would be. There is so much more to the past than many people realize. Not all black and white, good and bad."

"Oh, there's good and bad, believe me," Adam said in a low voice.

"Of course," Margot waved a hand as she explained herself. "Yes, please do not misunderstand. I simply mean that people can surprise us sometimes. Someone you might think is bad can do good things. People can hide the good things they do."

"Sometimes they have to." Adam agreed. "Mr. Bonnet is helping me now, too. I need to thank you for that recommendation as well."

"I'm pleased to hear it. He is not easy to deal with, I know." She smiled lightly.

"You're right about that. He's an odd one, for sure. I didn't think I could convince him at first. He reacted pretty badly when I approached him the first time."

"How so?" Margot's eyebrows furrowed. "He was angry?"

"Angry?" Adam was taken aback by the question. "I suppose he was. Which surprises me, I guess."

Margot shrugged. "He has his own opinions, you know."

"Yeah, and some history, too, I'm learning. Some violence in his past."

"Please don't take that too seriously," she said, placing a gentle hand on Adam's knee. "Don't read too much into this event from his youth."

Adam wasn't sure he shared her perspective. He knew

there were people who were violent, simply part of who they were.

"But you figured him out, I take it?" Margot was saying.

"I did, thanks. With a little help from a friend. Elise," he added when Margot looked at him quizzically. "She spoke to him on my behalf, convinced him I was worth helping, I guess."

"I see," Margot said in a tone Adam recognized.

"Nothing like that," he tried to stop where her mind was going. "She's just being helpful. That's all."

"M-hm," Margot's words said yes but her voice made it clear she didn't believe him for a second.

"I offered to help her in return," Adam found himself explaining. He hadn't planned to share his arrangement with Elise, but he needed to nip this rumor in the bud before it grew. "I'm helping her by talking to some of the townspeople about Thomas."

"About Thomas? Why?"

"I have some experience in dealing with murders, you know. I just offered to see what I could learn — without getting in the police's way, of course."

"Of course," Margot said dryly. "I'm sure they'll appreciate that."

Adam grinned at her attitude. She was giving him a tough time, but the smile that played at the corners of her lips made it clear she didn't mean it.

"Margot, *cherie.*" Julien swept into the waiting room and planted a kiss on his wife's cheek. "I am sorry you have had to wait." He placed a hand around her waist and turned to Adam. "Monsieur Kaminski, may I help you with something?"

Adam stood and shook the man's hand, avoiding the awkward kisses. "I need to report something I saw today."

"Yes? What is it?"

Apparently he expected Adam to speak to him in front of Margot. And didn't intend to take notes.

"I saw what I think is a weapon. In Sebastien's barn."

"What were you doing in Sebastien's barn?" Julien asked.

"I wasn't — in it, I mean." Adam paused, knowing how this would sound. "I was looking in the window."

Julien's brows went up in surprise. "I see."

"I know, it sounds strange. I was just looking around. Being nosy, I guess. And I saw a metal pipe — a part of an engine — lying on the ground of the barn."

"It is his workshop. That is not unusual."

"This was unusual. It wasn't put away, it wasn't cleaned off. And I'm pretty sure there was blood on it."

Julien shook his head and shrugged. "Monsieur Kaminski, this is nothing. A man bleeds when he cuts himself, doing his work, perhaps."

"I'm telling you, I know what I saw." Adam felt his anger rising. "I'm a good cop, you have to trust me on that. This wasn't blood from a cut. And it had some dried grass or something stuck to it."

"So you immediately think, what? A dirty tool, this man must be a killer?" Julien's voice rose with his anger. "You do not know Sebastien. You do not know anyone in this town. How dare you throw about accusations?"

"I'm not accusing anyone." Adam clenched his teeth to keep from shouting back, to keep his voice level. "But I do know that Sebastien has a temper. And he's a big enough guy to have been able to take on Thomas."

"Irrelevant," Julien snapped. "With the indication of drugs we found—" Julien stopped short, clearly realizing he'd said too much. He took a step back from Adam and closed his eyes for just a moment. When he opened his eyes, he blew out a breath, then spoke more calmly. "Monsieur Kaminski, even if I believe you — and frankly, I do not think I do — if you think this is connected to the murder of Thomas, well, as I said earlier, that is not my investigation. The *gendarmes* are here. If they want to talk to Sebastien — or you, for that matter — they will."

"Julien," Margot's quiet voice cut into the silence that followed Julien's pronouncement, the two men simply glaring at each other. "Julien, this is probably nothing," she glanced at Adam and smiled, "but it will not hurt to look, will it?"

Julien looked at her in surprise, as did Adam.

She raised one shoulder and gave Julien a look Adam didn't understand. "Go with Monsieur Kaminski. See what he is speaking about. Then," she held up a finger and turned to Adam, "then you can join us at our house for lunch. I am preparing a *bouillabaisse* and there is plenty of food."

Julien's face darkened and Adam fully expected an explosion. Instead, he let out a breath and laughed. "Of course, my dear, you are correct." He looked back at Adam. "Sometimes I let my anger make my decisions. You saw something that concerns you. I will go with you to take a look. And of course you must join us for lunch. We will be there shortly, my dear."

29

"Yes, I see what you mean," Julien admitted, looking around the otherwise orderly workspace.

Julien hadn't faced the same reluctance on entering the barn as Adam had. As he pointed out, the door was propped open and he had a reasonable suspicion based on Adam's complaints to at least look around.

He was not, however, willing to take it farther than that. He pulled out his phone and his conversation was brief and to the point. Hanging up, he turned around slowly, taking in the situation one more time.

"It stands out, doesn't it?" Adam asked.

"Indeed. We must consider the possibility it was placed there without Monsieur Roux's knowledge."

"Maybe," Adam walked closer to the part, keeping his hands in his pockets to avoid accidentally touching anything. "But it looks to me like he dropped it and then tried to hang up his jacket and it fell, covering it. I've seen Sebastien at night — he might not have been sober."

"No," Julien frowned. "That is a distinct possibility." He joined Adam next to the bloody piece of metal, leaning closer. "Those are *chélidoine*, a common weed, see the yellow flowers?"

Adam looked closer and saw a few yellow petals crushed into the grooves of the pipe. "If you say so, I wouldn't recognize them."

Julien straightened up. "They grow by the river. This may well be the weapon that was used to strike Monsieur Marchand." He walked along the wall, turning at the work-bench, making a circuit of the space. "I appreciate you bringing this to my attention, Monsieur Kaminski. This is important. But I do not think it is connected to the murder."

"What? You find a bloody pipe after a man's been beaten to death and you don't think it's connected?"

Julien raised one eyebrow, his head on the side. "It is a ... I don't know the word in English. A *biellette de direction*. The weapon will be tested, of course. I have called the *gendarmes* and they will examine it closely. But I tell you, that blood, those plants, those are not from the vineyard. Thomas was a fastidious farmer. He would not have allowed those weeds to grow on his farm, they are invasive. He would have destroyed them much earlier."

Adam glanced at the pipe then back at Julien, torn between being impressed that Julien knew so much about his town and frustrated that he could be ignoring the obvi-ous. "It could have been used on Thomas first, then later on Enzo. Same weapon."

Julien rolled his eyes. "Yes, I realize that. As I said, the *gendarmes* will examine it closely. They will talk with Monsieur Roux. Do not worry." He glanced at his watch. "This may take some time."

"For them to get here? They're still in town, aren't they?"

"*Oui*, of course. But I explained what we have, and they

must travel to Aix-en-Provence to get a warrant — *a mandat de perquisition* — to search this property officially." He shrugged. "I am afraid we will miss the lunch my wife promised you."

"Yeah, I guess so. So this is something else you have to turn over to the national police?"

"*Non*, if this is not connected to the murder, I will most likely be assigned to investigate. As a deputy of the mayor and in support of the *police judiciare*."

"Won't the police wonder what we were doing here, searching Sebastien's barn?" Adam asked.

A small grin crossed Julien's face. "I will simply explain that you and I were on our way to lunch and stopped by to see Sebastien about ... em ..." he paused, thinking, "... about something that needs fixing. A ceiling fan." He snapped his fingers as he came up with the suggestion.

Adam laughed. "Very creative. And believable. Alright, I'll wait with you."

"But we should not wait in here." Julien put a hand on Adam's arm to direct him back out of the barn. "Come, we will wait in front of the house."

Adam followed the other man along the stone path, back out to the street, and sat on the stone steps leading up to Sebastien's front door. The stone was warm in the sunshine and Adam leaned back, his elbows on the next step behind him.

"Comfortable?" Julien asked, shaking his head. "Americans."

Adam didn't even try to understand what Julien's complaint was about. It was clear he'd never truly under-stand French ways. He glanced around and saw Philippe Bonnet trundling in their direction, pulling a wire shopping basket behind him. The pavement was cracked, and every time the basket hit a crack it would bump up and down, its contents jumping along with it. Adam heard the jingle of glass and hoped Bonnet's purchases would arrive safely at home with him.

"*Bonjour,*" Julien greeted Bonnet as he passed in front of the house, touching his uniform hat in a respectful greeting.

Bonnet glared at him and shook his head. "Who do you harass now, eh?" His steps paused and he waved a hand toward Sebastien's house, the other hand still gripping tightly to his cart. "Why are you here? Because Sebastien is young? Angry? Pah," he waved the same hand, this time in derision. "He is one of the good ones, young Sebastien. You should leave him alone."

"I must do my job, Monsieur Bonnet. You know that. If we have questions—"

"Pah," Bonnet muttered again, cutting Julien off. Without another word, he continued his slow progress toward his house, his shopping bouncing along in the cart behind him.

Julien turned to Adam with a frown. "Perhaps it is good that I can leave this with the *gendarmes*. It is important to me that I have good relationships with the villagers."

"Makes sense," Adam said, leaning back again after sitting upright when Bonnet had approached.

Julien laughed and sat down next to Adam. "Perhaps the American way is correct this time. I will be comfortable as well. We may be waiting quite a while."

30

ELISE LOOKED up as she dragged a clean cloth across the last table top. She didn't know what made her look just then, but a second later and she would have missed it. A dark sedan passed by her window, the *Gendarme* logo on the front door. The car moved slowly, not part of an emergency, and as she looked, she recognized Sebastien in the back seat, a strange man sitting next to him.

She stood straight, startled. That was interesting. Andrew had been with Sebastien at the garage earlier that day. Had something happened? Or was Sebastien finally being held responsible for his many reckless acts?

She ran back to the kitchen, swung open the small wooden door and shouted up the stairs. "Andrew! Andrew!" She got no response, heard no creaking floorboards, no running water. She said it again, quieter, worried. "Andrew?"

She turned a questioning gaze to Henri, who shrugged. "I have not seen Monsieur Martin for over an hour."

Elise pulled the apron from around her waist and

grabbed a jacket from the hook. "I'll be back," she called as she ran out the door and headed for the police station.

Her breath came in short bursts and she could feel her heart pounding as she dashed through the streets toward the police station. Had Andrew been with Sebastien? Had they done something terrible?

Try as she might, she couldn't keep the tortured images out of her mind, driving herself faster to find the truth.

Throwing herself against the door, she charged into the police station, her mouth opening, ready to speak.

Julien, in the middle of saying something to Camille, cut himself off and turned to stare at her.

"Monsieur Roche, Mademoiselle Lambert," she took a few breaths, "is Andrew here?" Even as she asked the question, she felt her adrenaline dropping, her hands starting to shake. Fear was taking over.

"Mademoiselle Martin," Julien spoke calmly but couldn't — or didn't bother to — hide the irritation in his voice. "I will tell you the same thing I said to Mademoiselle Lambert, you must allow us to do our jobs. Please." He gestured to the bench, his eyes kind but his voice firm.

Both women sank meekly onto the seat. Julien nodded once, then disappeared into his office. Elise could hear voices when he opened the door, but they faded into an indistinct blur as soon as the door clicked shut.

She turned to Camille. "I saw they had Sebastien."

Camille nodded and Elise realized she'd been crying. "Oh, Camille, I am so sorry. Is there anything I can do to help?"

Camille shook her head and sniffed. "They will not let me talk with him. I don't know what they are asking him, what they are doing with him."

"Well," Elise let out a long sigh. "I suppose this is about Thomas, don't you think?"

Camille caught her breath in a sob. "That is ridiculous. Sebastien is not involved in that."

"No." Elise tried to make it sound like a statement, but she knew she didn't believe it. Camille could tell as well.

She jumped up, pushing Elise's proffered hand away. "You are glad! You are relieved they think Sebastien killed Thomas because it means your brother is innocent."

"No Camille." Elise stood too. "I am not glad. Please, believe me. This is a terrible tragedy. There is no joy in it for anyone. But how can we know...?"

Camille was beyond consolation. "You think he did this, this horrible thing? How could you? Do you think so little of me, of my judgment?"

"I'm so sorry, I should have thought." Elise shook her head, trying to find the right words.

"Well, he didn't do this murder. He did not kill Thomas."

"Camille, are you really so sure?"

"Of course. Sebastien was at work early that morning, the morning Thomas was killed. He was working on a big project that came in the night before and needed urgent work. His coworkers can vouch for him."

Of course, that's exactly what he would tell Camille, wouldn't he? But she was wise enough to keep that thought to herself.

"Camille, I am so glad to hear it. Happy for you and for Sebastien. Believe me."

Camille sniffed again and Elise pulled a pack of tissues from her jacket pocket. "Please, sit down."

This time Camille agreed, dabbing at her eyes. "You do not need to stay," she finally said. "Andrew is not here."

"Are you sure?"

Camille nodded. "Sebastien is in there. Alone. I don't know where Andrew is."

Elise patted her hand and waited with her friend. She didn't need to run off, and Camille clearly needed the support. But she wouldn't wait too long to find Adam. Someone needed to find out if Sebastien really was working early that morning.

31

PHILIPPE BONNET HADN'T MADE it far, trundling slowly with his loaded shopping cart. Adam tracked him down easily enough after leaving Julien with the *gendarmes* at Sebastien's barn. He had almost caught up with him when the older man stopped abruptly. Another figure appeared from around a corner and for a moment the two old men faced each other, each blocking the other from moving forward on the path.

Confused, Adam jogged toward them, assuming they must have stopped to talk. But as he approached, he realized they weren't talking. They were glaring.

Without saying a word, Bonnet let his anger show through his narrowed eyes and reddening face. The other man reacted just as strongly. Neither man moved, neither willing, apparently, to make way for the other.

Adam watched for a second or two, then figured he'd better jump in or those two men would be standing there for days.

"Excuse me, Monsieur Bonnet?" he asked.

Both men directed their glares to him. It took a moment

before the light of recognition appeared in Bonnet's eyes and he greeted Adam.

"I don't believe we've had the opportunity to meet yet." Adam extended a hand to the other man, who looked at it briefly before shaking it.

"Pah!" Bonnet spat out the word, literally. A drop of spittle landed on the other man's coat, leaving a dark mark.

Adam took a step closer, forcing his way between the two men. "Is there a problem here I can help with?"

"Help?" The other man asked. "You?" He laughed and stepped out into the street, around Adam and Monsieur Bonnet. Adam heard him still laughing as he continued down the street.

"What was that about?" Adam turned back to Bonnet. "Who was that?"

"*Putain.*" Bonnet directed the curse to the other man's retreating back. "Dubois."

"Monsieur Dubois?" Adam repeated the name. "I've heard that name before."

"Monsieur?" Bonnet sneered. "I wouldn't call him that. Just Dubois is good enough for him. For his family."

"They supported the Vichy regime, didn't they? His ancestors, I mean."

Bonnet glanced at Adam, then looked quickly away. "You do not know what things are like here, young man." He shook his head sadly. "You shake hands with a traitor without even thinking about it."

"A traitor?" Adam asked, surprised, joining Bonnet as the old man continued on his way. "He can hardly be a traitor. He's too young."

Bonnet shrugged and raised an eyebrow. "He is a Dubois. That is all I need to know."

Adam looked down at the sidewalk, considering. It

didn't seem fair to blame this man for his parents — or perhaps even grandparents — deeds. On the other hand, this was a small town, many people had been killed. He could understand why emotions would still run high.

"I was wondering," he asked, changing the topic, "if you'd had time to look into the history of Witold Kaminski yet."

Bonnet didn't look up at him but Adam saw a movement that could have been a small smile. "Have I had the time? Young man, I have nothing but time, now that I am retired."

Adam waited, knowing the man would say more when he felt like it. After a minute or so, he did.

"Do not pester me." Bonnet said. "I will find you when I have information for you."

Adam laughed under his breath. "I'm sure you will," he said softly, so softly the other man didn't hear him. In a louder voice, Adam added, "I'm very interested in your research, you know. I understand that you're retired from teaching, but I hope you still keep up your research."

"Oh yes?" Bonnet raised his eyebrows, which Adam took to be an expression of interest.

"I used to be a historian myself," Adam went on. "I was a teacher, too. I taught history."

Now Bonnet stopped and looked at Adam. "You are a history teacher? In the United States?"

Adam raised one hand, "I was. I left the field to become a cop." When Bonnet frowned, he added, "a police officer."

"Ahh," Bonnet continued his slow march toward his house. "You are an officer of the law."

Adam suspected this didn't endear him to the old man, so he went on. "I've been doing some research of my own. In the library at Cavaillon."

"The new *Mediatheque?*" Bonnet asked. He moved his head from side to side. "They are not bad. But they are very limited in what they offer. But," he held up one finger, "they are useful for getting documents from good resources. From Paris, for example. For this kind of research, we need government documents. Resistance documents. Original sources, not books about books."

"I read your book," Adam said. "At least, I started it. I'm still working through it."

"Oh?" Bonnet stopped again and gave Adam a more searching look. "You are reading it?" A smile flashed across the man's face, so quick Adam almost missed it, immediately replaced by the man's typical scowl.

Adam nodded. "I plan to go back to Cavaillon soon, to do more research. Unless you find something else — or somewhere else I should go."

Bonnet shrugged. "This is a good place for you, I think. They will be able to help you. I, on the other hand, I have my contacts. Old colleagues. In Paris, in Avignon. I review primary sources, you understand. Diaries. Letters."

"Like the letters I showed you."

Bonnet nodded again. "Indeed. They are a very good resource. Do not pester me," he said again, but this time his voice was kinder. "I will find out what I can."

Adam stopped following him, letting the old man continue his slow progress down the street. He had to find Elise, let her know what he'd found in Sebastien's barn.

32

ONCE AGAIN, Adam found himself standing outside the metal door with a plaque proclaiming *Bertrand Garage et Pièces Auto* — Bertrand Garage and Auto Supplies — in bold gold letters. Unlike the last time, however, he opened the door.

Bertrand's professional garage was only slightly larger than Sebastien's barn. Two closed bay doors made up most of the back wall and two vehicles filled the space in front of the doors. One vehicle, a sedan, sat alone, but the other had its hood propped open. The bottom halves of two men stuck out from the engine, their heads buried within.

"Hello. *Bonjour*," Adam called as he walked past the car toward the small truck the men were fixing. As he passed the car, he recognized a pipe — a *biellette de direction* — lying to the side. The same as the part he'd just seen covered in somebody's blood.

"*Oui monsieur?*" One man straightened up as he responded. The other man glanced at him over his shoulder, then went back to work.

Adam fumbled in French for a moment before the

young man cut him off. "Please monsieur, I speak in English, if that is easier for you?"

"Thank you, it is. I'm here because Sebastien Roux has been arrested, I don't know if you heard?"

"We did." The man leaned heavily with both hands on the side of the car, his face expressing the same disappointment as his voice. "This left us shorthanded today. Police are being ridiculous, he would never kill anyone."

The other mechanic, an older man whose dark and roughened skin suggested years spent poking around under and in cars, turned to stare at Adam but said nothing, perhaps not knowing enough English.

"So you think he was arrested for the murder?" Adam asked.

"Of course, what else?" The man looked confused and said a few quick words in French to his colleague, who laughed.

"But I understand he was here the morning of the murder," Adam said.

The young man threw his hands in the air, his voice rising. "Of course he was, and when the police ask us we will tell them that."

"Was he here all morning?" Adam asked quickly. "From what time?"

"Monsieur, Sebastien was in before the sun was up. I do not know what time poor Thomas was killed, but I can tell you Sebastien was here early and working hard."

"All morning?" Adam pressed.

The older man muttered something and the young man nodded. "Indeed. More so than some. I went out to get us some fresh bread and saw even Nico was getting into work later." He spoke again in French and both men grinned. "No, that is not like him at all."

When the young man saw Adam wasn't joining in the joke, he rubbed his fingers together in the universal symbol for money.

"Ah," Adam said and tried to generate a smile. "So you're sure, then?"

"*Oui.*" The young man rolled his eyes toward the older, who grunted and turned his back to Adam, bending down and grabbing something within the engine.

Adam wasn't quite ready to let them go. "That ... that pipe." He pointed at the part that had attracted his attention earlier. "A *biellette de direction.*"

"Yes?" The men once again stood and stared at him.

"What is that?"

"What is it?" They spoke rapidly to each other in French, then the young man turned back to Adam. "In English, a tie rod."

Adam nodded. "I've heard of that. It supports alignment, right? Makes sure the suspension is solid?"

The mechanic frowned as he nodded. "*Oui,* that is about it. Why do you ask?"

"Why is that there?"

The man shrugged, obviously baffled by the question. "It is broken and had to be replaced. Someone brought it over and exchanged it for a new one."

"Who?" Adam took a step toward the man.

He lowered his brows. "Sebastien. Why do you ask this?"

Adam didn't offer a response, only another question. "Where did this broken tie rod come from?"

The men spoke to each other again, both shaking their heads and gesturing toward the broken tie rod.

"We do not know. Monsieur, we must get back to work. There is no more we can add."

The older man resumed his position within the truck's engine, the younger put his hands on his hips and stared at Adam. He was clearly no longer welcome here.

He had a few answers, but even more questions. Could Sebastien's coworkers be trusted to tell the truth or were they protecting Sebastien? Why did he have a bloody tie rod in his possession? And most importantly, did Sebastien use that tie rod to kill Thomas?

33

"Andrew, thank God. Where have you been?" Elise dropped the sponge she was holding into the sink and ran to Andrew, trying to wrap her arms around him.

"I'm fine, I'm fine." He pushed her away with a shrug. "I was just out with some friends."

Elise stepped back and looked at him closely. After so many years of taking care of him, she recognized the look in his eyes. "You heard about Sebastien?"

"Yeah, I heard," Andrew slumped against a counter, his face grim. "The cops here are a joke. No way Sebastien did that."

Elise didn't share his confidence in his friend, but now was not the time to tell him. "If he's innocent, they'll figure it out. I'm sure of it."

He gave her a wry glance. "Really? You trust those jerks from the *gendarmes*?"

She could only shrug and offer him a small smile.

"Maybe if it was Julien, he's at least reasonable," Andrew continued. "He knows us, knows this town." He shook his head and stood tall, his eyes more sad than angry now. "I don't know what's going on around here. I'm going out to get some food."

"Come on." Elise tapped his arm gently, before he could resist. "Come upstairs, I'll make you dinner."

He followed her quietly up the two flights of stairs, the only sound the creak of the old steps and his heavy tread behind her. She risked a glance back at him only once, worried his mood would shift again.

In their apartment, he slumped at the kitchen table while Elise pulled together some bread, cheese and leftover meat pie, pouring out a glass of red wine for him as she did so. He sipped the wine and watched her work.

"Why are you doing this?" he asked.

"What? Making us dinner?" She smiled as she asked and finished plating their small meal.

"Taking care of me. Mothering me." He shook his head. "You always take care of me."

"You're my brother," she said as she put the plate in front of him and slid into a chair across the table from him. She leaned over to the counter to grab the bottle of wine and pour herself a glass. "I'll always take care of you."

His eyes darkened and he tore off a piece of bread. "You shouldn't."

She didn't answer, knowing what he was thinking. Knowing how different her life would be right now if she hadn't chosen to take care of him. To put him first, before anything else.

"And what are you doing with that cop? From the States?"

She shrugged. "He's a nice enough man. Why shouldn't I be spending time with him?"

Andrew laughed. "Is that what you want me to think?

That you're just hanging out with him because you like him?"

She raised a questioning eyebrow as she put a piece of the meat pie on her plate.

"No," he said. "I know you're worried about Thomas' murder. You're interfering in the investigation."

"Why do you say that?"

"I saw you yesterday. With the cop. Walking over to Thomas' farm. I know what you're doing, Elise."

"Alright, it's true." She chose her words carefully. "I just wanted to see if there was anything I could do to help. Like you said, the *gendarmes* don't know this town. I do. And Adam is a cop, he knows about investigating."

"So you think you're helping?"

She shrugged again. "I don't know. But I don't want anything bad to happen."

"Bad? Thomas is dead. What could be worse?"

"I don't want the wrong person blamed," she said quietly.

His anger surprised her, even after all these years. He slammed a hand onto the table as he stood, spilling his wine. "Well the wrong person has been blamed, hasn't he?"

He stomped out to the front door, then stomped back to add, "Sebastien didn't kill anyone. I know it. You need to stop getting in the way and let the cops do their job."

She sat still, frozen as he slammed the door behind him. Heaven forgive her, but she hoped beyond hope that Sebastien was guilty. Because if he wasn't, she didn't dare think about who else the police would arrest.

34

THE YOUNG MECHANIC left the garage at six. Adam watched from a spot down the street, where he'd been waiting for the past thirty minutes, hoping the man would leave promptly at the garage's posted closing time. The man said something over his shoulder as the door closed behind him, presumably to the older man still in the office, then headed in Adam's direction. Adam moved away from him, picking up his pace so that he could turn a corner and get out of the young man's line of sight.

He watched from a doorway as the man continued straight, then fell into step behind him. His goal was to get the young mechanic alone, out of his work environment and away from his boss. He still had lots of questions about Sebastien and he was pretty sure this young man had some of the answers.

Adam thanked his luck when he headed into Nico's *tabac*.

Lingering a few minutes before following him in, Adam watched as other patrons came and left, some hanging around outside smoking. The familiar gang of teenagers approached, then moved quickly away. Adam wondered who they'd seen to make them change their direction.

Eventually, Adam went in and propped himself up at the bar. In response to Nico's questioning glance, he ordered a beer.

"No interest in our local wine then?" Nico asked, his voice friendly. "Or you could try a *pastis*, that's very traditional in this part of France."

Adam glanced at the young man he'd been following, who was standing at the far end of the bar downing his own beer.

"Just a beer for tonight, thanks Nico."

Nico shrugged and pulled the beer. Adam took a sip, considering his best approach.

He knew he shouldn't only focus on Sebastien. There were clearly other people in the village with motive who had the opportunity to kill Thomas. But something about Sebastien set off Adam's radar. The man was cruel and Adam had no doubt he could be pushed too far. But he knew better than to jump to conclusions without any real evidence. And that meant getting test results that connected that tie rod to Thomas' murder — a task that only Julien or the *gendarmes* could do — and finding the weakness in Sebastien's alibi.

Adam picked up his beer and walked over to the young mechanic. "Thanks for talking with me earlier."

The young man looked up, surprised. "Ah yes, the American."

"Adam Kaminski." Adam put out his hand. "I don't think I properly introduced myself before."

The young man frowned but shook his hand. "Claude Deloire," he introduced himself grudgingly.

Adam leaned against the bar next to him and gestured to Claude's empty beer glass. "Can I buy you another?"

Claude lowered his brows but nodded and Adam signaled to Nico.

"I haven't seen you around before." Adam said once Claude had his beer. "Are you a friend of Sebastien's?"

Claude glared at Adam over his beer glass, then put the glass down forcefully on the bar. "Why are you asking these questions? I told you earlier, Sebastien was at work the morning Thomas died. Why do you care?"

Claude's voice was rising so Adam leaned back a bit to give the young man more breathing space. He took a sip of his own beer and shrugged casually. "Sorry, I shouldn't be prying. Elise asked me to check into things." He paused, watching Claude's reaction, then added, "for Andrew."

Claude looked quickly at Adam. "Why is Andrew concerned? Because he is a friend of Sebastien?"

Adam shrugged again. "I suppose."

Claude took another drink then wiped his mouth with the back of a hand. Adam hoped he'd accepted Adam's spin on the situation.

"Have you told the police yet, that Sebastien was working that morning?"

Claude nodded but lowered his brows. "Imbeciles," he grumbled under his breath. "What do they know?"

Adam chuckled and refrained from defending his French colleagues. To be fair, he had no idea what they knew. "So that's good then, right? They'll have to accept that."

"Pah," Claude almost spit into his beer, speaking as he took another drink. "They care about only one thing."

Adam waited, hoping for more, giving Claude time express his anger.

Claude continued, "I mentioned that Sebastien was worried about finishing the job, that it was important to him, that he wouldn't risk it."

Adam nodded, making a small sound of agreement but nothing more.

"He even got angry when Monsieur Bertrand required him to deliver a car that had been repaired," Claude said.

Adam tried not to show his reaction on his face. "He didn't want to leave the garage?"

"*Précisément!*" Claude snapped his fingers. "But he did it anyway, so quickly. Out and back, just like that."

"And the *gendarmes* know about this?"

"Imbeciles." Claude repeated. "They think this is significant. But how can it be? He was gone no more than ten minutes." Claude let out a deep breath as he shook his head, then drained his glass.

Adam raised a hand to Nico and ordered another round for both of them.

Claude raised the glass in a salute of thanks when it arrived and downed half in one go. Apparently the young man was just getting started on his evening. But Adam had a few more questions before he could let the man drink in peace.

"Sebastien was no friend of Thomas, was he?" Adam asked, keeping his voice casual.

Fortunately, the beer seemed to be kicking in and dampening Claude's suspicious nature. "Why should he be?" he asked.

Adam shrugged and shook his head. "I hear no one was very close to him." When Claude gave him a look, Adam added. "Other than Andrew and Elise, of course."

"*Exactement,*" Claude snapped his fingers again.

"Thomas was ..." Claude rolled his eyes around as if looking for the word in his head.

"Difficult." Adam supplied.

Claude smiled and raised one finger. "*Oui*. Oh yes. That man liked to lord it over everyone else. As if his family, just because they own the big farm, are somehow better than the rest of us. Look at the way he accepts gifts from villagers."

"I heard something about that. Why was that? I mean, why did people make him food or give him small gifts?"

Claude raised one eyebrow, lifted a shoulder. He knew something he wasn't sharing, that much was clear. Then he continued, "But we know his family's history. We know how they got that farm. We won't forget."

"They made their money during the war." Adam prodded him. "People got hurt because of them."

Claude nodded. "We won't forget," he repeated. "Seb would never forget."

"He hated Thomas?"

"Hate? No." Claude lowered his brow as he shook his head. "No, not hate. But there was something about the way he reacted whenever he saw Thomas. Hate? No. But perhaps ..." Claude frowned. "Perhaps fear."

35

Light shone from only a few windows of the school building. Most of the staff and teachers had left hours earlier. Passing on the far side of the street, Adam didn't think anything of it until he saw a form moving in one of the lit rooms. A form he easily recognized as Margot Roche.

Changing directions, he jogged across the street and into the school. Margot jumped when he knocked on the frame of her open door.

"Sorry, I didn't mean to scare you. Do you have time to chat?" he asked.

"Of course, Monsieur Kaminski. Come in, I am just packing up to go home."

"Late night?"

She made a face. "It is not unusual. There is always something. Now, I work with the students on a small performance."

"That's great," Adam said with feeling. "I always loved the extra activities, when the kids were there because they were interested, because they enjoyed what we were doing."

Margot smiled. "But you do not enjoy what you do now?"

Adam shrugged and sat down at one of the student desks. The chair groaned loudly and when Margot's eyes widened, he stood up. "Sorry, won't hold my weight I guess." He leaned against the wall instead, crossing his arms in front of him.

"How can I help you, Monsieur Kaminski?" she asked.

"I don't know." Adam looked around the room as he spoke. "I've been walking back and forth around town, seeing how long it takes me to get from the garage to Thomas' farm and from the town out to the river ..."

Margot laughed kindly. "Why are you doing this?"

"Just trying to break an alibi." He shook his head. "An unbreakable alibi, apparently." He took a deep breath and let it out slowly. "I'm missing something, but I don't know what."

He'd found a bloody pipe. A tie rod clearly belonging to Sebastien, a rod he'd seen him carrying, a rod now covered in blood. If the blood matched Thomas', that sort of evidence was usually conclusive.

"I am sorry you are frustrated." Margot turned her attention back to her bag as she shoved even more notebooks into it. It was already bulging, but she still managed to fit more in. "Perhaps your other personal investigation is going better?" She paused to look at him.

He shrugged again. "Perhaps. Mr. Bonnet is doing some research for me, which is good. And thank you," he put a hand out without touching her. "Thank you again for what you did for me. I can't tell you how much I valued meeting those people, hearing their stories."

Her face glowed, matching his enthusiasm. "I am so

pleased. And not surprised. I knew you would understand the value of learning about the past. About our culture."

Adam nodded, thinking. "So is that what I'm missing in this murder investigation? Knowledge about this town, about France?"

She offered a broad shrug. "Perhaps. We in France are not like you in the States. We think differently. We do things differently." She hefted the bag onto her shoulder, then after a moment put it back down on her desk. "Why do people kill other people, Monsieur Kaminski?"

Adam thought about it. "Fear." He moved his head side to side. "Greed, definitely." He thought some more. "And love."

"Love?" she asked with surprise.

"Sure. Love can lead to all kinds of problems. Jealousy. Hatred. Who knows what?"

But mostly it came down to money, he knew. So many reasons to kill, but so often it was for greed. Because someone wanted more. Could it be that simple here, too? Or was this really about the past, the Vichy regime? Or about food? Or wine? Or farming?

She looked down at her hands. "I'm so sorry you have to work with these types of people. And grateful that this is not more common here. Julien—"

"Julien what?"

Why didn't someone coming down that hallway make more noise, Adam thought to himself as he stood straight at Julien's entrance into the room.

Margot made a small sound of surprise as she walked to her husband and kissed his cheeks. "Darling, why are you here?"

"I saw the light on and came to carry your bag," he said, glancing at Adam. "Am I interrupting?"

"Not at all," Adam said. "I was just tossing out some ideas. Your wife thinks I need to learn more about your town, your culture." He didn't add that this would help him in investigating the murder. He wasn't sure how pleased Julien would be to hear he was still pursuing it.

"Of course you must." Julien opened his arms wide. "Our history. Our music. Our wine. Our food." He looked pointedly at his wife. "You must be hungry."

She laughed out loud. "I am not, but I know you are."

"Yes." He shot Adam a look of mock anger. "Since I was required to miss my lunch today."

"Come," Margot said, handing her husband the heavy shoulder bag. "Come home and I will let you feed me."

Adam laughed. "Are you a cook, Julien?"

"Why not?" he retorted. "My quiche is legendary." He slung the bag over his shoulder. "But seriously, if you are interested in our town, then understanding our way of life is important. In fact, please, join us for dinner. Since you also missed your lunch."

Adam accepted the invitation gladly, and not just for the food. Margot was right that he needed to learn more about this town and its residents. And who better to learn details from than the chief of police?

36

ELISE'S STEP faltered as she entered the *tabac*, not sure if she was hoping to see Andrew or hoping he wasn't there. It had been over an hour, his anger should have cleared by now. But the last thing he'd want was her following him. She stopped in the doorway and looked around the space.

Nico stood behind the bar, drying a glass with the towel he always seemed to have handy, saying something to Philippe Bonnet, who sat sipping a *pastis*. Philippe's presence surprised her. He wasn't a regular here as far as she knew. She nodded a greeting to Nico and Phillippe as she passed the bar to stick her head around the far wall and confirm that Andrew wasn't at one of the tables in the back. Once she was sure he wasn't there, she relaxed against the bar.

"Monsieur Bonnet," she said, "it's a pleasure to see you taking a break from your research."

"Hm," the man responded curtly. He raised one eyebrow at Nico, as if to say, "see what I mean?" Elise had no idea what he meant, so she turned her attention to Nico, ordering a wine.

"I hear that Enzo is doing well," Nico said casually.

"Yes, I'm so relieved." Elise took a sip of her wine. "Back to his old self, I hope."

Nico grinned. "He hasn't made it back here, yet. We miss him, don't we, Philippe?" Nico raised his voice to include the other man in the comment, but Philippe ignored it. "At least we're not short of grumpy old men." He laughed as he insulted Philippe, who finally spoke up.

"I am not grumpy. I came here for companionship, after all. I simply choose not to speak when I have nothing important to say."

"Nonsense, you always have important information, Monsieur Bonnet. How is your latest work going? I understand you've been involved with research into the French Popular Party during the war. Is that right?" Elise asked.

Philippe nodded. "I am. I must make sure that everyone knows about their activities, their crimes. To keep the memories alive. We cannot forget what those bastards did."

"The war is long over, old man," Nico's words were harsh but he spoke kindly. "Why do you get so worked up about it?"

Philippe glared at him. "If you had been alive. If you had seen what they did. You would not make light of it."

"But you weren't alive then, were you?"

Philippe shrugged. "Pah. That is not the point. I remember the stories my parents told me. I remember how destroyed they were, our town, our country."

"And have you found out anything more about Adam Kaminski's ancestor?" Elise asked.

Philippe nodded. "I have. You were correct, Madame. He was one of the good ones."

"I'm so glad. How did you find the information?"

Philippe, apparently finally finding a topic of conversation worthy of his participation, launched into a long explanation of the process through which the library in the town of Avignon was able to request documents from the *Bibliothèque Nationale de France*.

Nico, who had stepped away to serve another customer during Philippe's explanation, returned his attention to his friends. "So not everyone during the war was bad, then."

"Of course not. So many people fought on the side of right." Philippe shook his head. "So many people died. Look at poor Sebastien and his family." His voice faded away.

Elise and Nico shared a glance but said nothing. Eventually, Philippe said again. "He's one of the good ones, Sebastien. They should not be treating him like that."

"I'm sure he's being treated very well," Elise tried to reassure him. "The police these days are professionals, you know that."

"Pah," Philippe muttered, "what do they know? They think a man like Sebastien could harm someone else. Never."

Elise shook her head in amazement. She'd seen Sebastien in drunken rages often enough to know how wrong Philippe was.

Yet ... there was something in what he was saying. She slowly sipped her wine and wondered. Sebastien hadn't killed Thomas, not if he was at work at that time of the murder. Even with the new fact that he had left the garage briefly, Adam said there still wasn't time for him to run up to Thomas' farm, kill him and run back to the garage.

She let out a breath and looked around the bar. Nico quietly wiped down glasses. Philippe scowled over his drink. He was so adamant that Sebastien was a good man. She shook her head and took another drink. Then she frowned. Andrew was right. She was at least partly to blame for Sebastien's arrest. If she hadn't asked Adam to get involved, he wouldn't have gone to Sebastien's barn and found the weapon. And Sebastien wouldn't be in jail now.

This was her fault. She'd been so eager to help Andrew she'd become involved in something she didn't understand. Something she couldn't understand. She should never have asked Adam to look into the murder. No matter who had done it — or where Andrew had been at the time. She finished her wine and put her glass down firmly, nodding to Nico and Philippe as she left the *tabac* with a new sense of determination. She needed to find a way to fix things.

37

"Come in, come in." Philippe Bonnet's enthusiasm at seeing Adam at his front door so early in the morning surprised Adam.

"*Bonjour monsieur,*" he said. "It's good to see you again."

"Yes, yes," the old man said impatiently. "I have been doing some research, come see."

He turned his back on Adam and trotted up the stairs. Adam followed a few steps back, taking off his coat as he walked and draping it over his arm.

Upstairs, Philippe kept up his pace down a long hallway carpeted in a narrow, threadbare runner. The Fleur de Lis pattern matched the colors of the wallpaper but clashed with the portraits hanging at odd intervals along the wall.

"Your family?" Adam asked of the portraits, but Philippe ignored him, obviously already focused on what he'd found in his research.

He led them to a room at the far end of the hall overlooking the back garden. A beige cloth covered the round table in the center of the room, three chairs tipped forward toward the table. A fourth chair sat flat, pulled away as if Philippe had just jumped up. A conclusion strengthened when he plopped back down into it and pulled an old photo album toward him.

"Come, look," he said impatiently.

Adam pulled out a chair and sat next to him, leaning to look over Philippes's shoulder. "Who am I looking at?"

The album was open to a page holding three photographs. Posed shots, they each portrayed a group of people with various degrees of scowls. Adam knew that a couple of generations ago it had not been fashionable to smile in photographs, but this group seemed to be taking that edict to heart. Even the children frowned.

Two pictures showed the same couple, a middle-aged man and woman in what might have been their Sunday best. She wore a tweed skirt suit, probably in a dark color, based on the way it looked in the black and white photo. He wore trousers, shirt and blazer, the blazer hanging a little looser that it should. Whether because it had been bought second hand or the man had been losing weight, Adam couldn't know. A gaggle of kids appeared in each photo, but to Adam's eye they looked like different children in each picture.

The third photo showed only the woman, with two more children.

"This," Philippe said triumphantly, jabbing his finger at the page next to the first two photos, "is Monsieur Louvois."

He said it like it meant something, and Adam wracked his brain trying to remember if he'd encountered the name at any point in his visit, perhaps during his lunch meeting yesterday. He came up blank. He shook his head.

"Ach!" Philippe threw up his hands in disgust. "I was

told you met with some of the townspeople who descended from these children. Did they not tell you?"

He had no reason, but Adam felt guilty for not recognizing the name. "I'm sorry, if they did I do not remember it."

"Pah," Philippe waved this idea away with his hand. "You would have remembered. They did not mention it. To their shame."

"Who was he?" Adam asked softly.

"He was the teacher." He looked squarely at Adam, a smile in his eyes.

At that moment, Adam knew.

He knew exactly who Monsieur Louvois was. He knew what he meant. "He was the teacher," he repeated, a smile growing on his face.

Philippe beamed. "Yes. This man," he jabbed at the photo again. "This man worked with someone from beyond the border, someone in Germany or Poland or ... or somewhere. He got the children out, got them to Switzerland."

Adam took a breath and sat back in his chair. This was the man. The man who had worked with his own great-grandfather. The man with whom his great-grandfather had exchanged letters, letters written in code so the Nazis couldn't understand them.

"This is it, then. This is the proof. My great-grandfather was a teacher as well. In Poland. They worked together."

"This, well ..." Philippe shrugged broadly as he frowned. "This I cannot say. The person he worked with across the border was never known."

"He never said, never told anyone?"

Philippe shook his head. "How could he? Why would he? It was too dangerous. It didn't matter." He shook his head as he stared down at the photos.

"Didn't matter? It matters to me." Adam felt his voice rising.

"No, you misunderstand. All that secrecy, all that care, it wasn't enough." He shook his head again. "He was killed. By traitors."

Adam looked at Philippe then looked again at the photos. "Someone killed him?"

"Someone? No." Philippe shook his head. "Not someone. The Nazis killed him. Monsters, not people. But the *putain* who turned him in. Yes, he killed him just as much as the Nazis did."

"Do you know who that was?" Adam realized he was whispering and coughed to clear his throat.

"Oh yes, it is well known. The Lefebvres practically ran this town during the Vichy regime. They knew everything. And they sold everything, everyone. For power. For money." Philippe's voice faded out, but his hands shook as he leaned on the table and his face grew red. "They sold out their people, their country. They have no heart. No morality. They are not French." His voice rose as he spoke until he shouted out the last word.

Adam stood, paced around the room.

"So the Lefebvres turned in the person they knew to be helping Jewish children. He was killed because of them."

"*Oui.*"

"Did no one help?"

"Of course." Philippe stood as well, his anger rising again. "You think everyone in this town was a traitor? A coward?"

"No, no," Adam put his hands up and stepped toward the old man, hoping to calm him.

Philippe moved away from him, turning to stare at a painting of a river, maybe the river in this town. Adam looked at the painting, and saw the signature in the bottom corner. "A. Roux."

"The Roux family," Philippe said out loud. "They fought. They fought like animals when they had to." The words seemed harsh, but Philippe said them with pride. "We know. We tell the stories, we hold on to the memories. The Roux," he turned back to Adam. "My own family, others. They fought back in any way they could."

He returned to the table and slowly, carefully slid into a chair as if all his energy had been spent. "They made problems, caused problems, delays, errors. Anything to stop those in power. And they killed. Oh yes," he glanced up at Adam. "When necessary, they killed." He shook his head. "But it wasn't enough."

"Perhaps it was," Adam sat next to the old man. "Some died, true." He looked down at the photo of Monsieur Louvois. "But the Nazis were defeated. They lost. You won."

Philippe dipped his head, in acknowledgment though not agreement. "He had no children of his own, it seems," he added.

"Monsieur Louvois?"

Philippe nodded. "No one to carry on his story. And that those people you met yesterday didn't mention him. That is ... I can't ..." Adam realized Philippe was crying, silent tears sliding down his wrinkled cheeks.

He sat silently, nothing to add.

So Sebastien's family had been fighters. Great resistance fighters, apparently. Did that mean he was wrong about Sebastien? With ancestors like that, could he really be a killer?

Adam laughed softly to himself, then glanced at

Philippe to make sure the old man didn't think he was laughing at him, but Philippe's attention was elsewhere.

Adam couldn't let himself fall for that trick. Just because his parents and grandparents were good people didn't mean that Sebastien was, too. He may have been raised on stories of these ancestors. Stories of fighting, of killing. And yet ... Adam looked over at the old man, still silently crying as he looked through the photographs. Had he been too quick to judge?

38

Market day in *Saint-Honoré* meant the paved lot not far from the town center filled with vans, carts and trucks selling everything from onions to overalls. Adam absorbed the pungent scents of the local Banon cheese and pork sausages, felt the rough wool of the scarves hanging from one tent and the soft cotton of T-shirts in another. Amazed at the variety of goods on sale in a town so small, Adam wandered past every vendor, touching, smelling, even tasting samples. He knew his impression of the market was flavored by his excitement over what he'd learned from Philipe Bonnet, but nevertheless this was an exceptional small town market.

He recognized Elise's voice as he turned the corner around a meat van and stepped past the geese and ducks hanging from the van's raised flap to see her two carts down the aisle, engaged in what seemed to be a serious discussion at a vegetable stall. After much pointing, exclaiming and squeezing of produce, Elise accepted her parcels and handed over an agreed sum.

Adam approached as she negotiated. As soon as she

completed her purchase, he spoke to get her attention and offered her the standard kisses that he was beginning to feel more comfortable about. "What a great way to shop. I know I'd eat better if I had a market like this in Philly."

Elise smiled up at him in greeting. "Yes, this market moves from town to town, you know. People come from around the countryside to sell their goods. We have some regulars," she waved her hand toward the vendor she had just left, "but always some new choices as well." She stopped in front of a cart selling soaps and candles, sniffing at a few of the candles, but not buying anything.

"And you have this every week?"

"Of course," Elise laughed. "Don't sound so surprised. We're a small village, sure, but we still need to shop."

They walked together past a few more stalls. Adam took the opportunity to buy a new scarf and a pair of gloves, figuring he'd need them for the Philly winter.

"I'm glad I ran into you, actually," Elise spoke casually as Adam paid for his purchases. "I wanted to let you know that I don't want to waste any more of your time on something that should stay with the police."

Adam, who had leaned forward to examine some books laid out on a table, straightened with surprise. "You don't want to keep looking into who killed Thomas?"

Elise shook her head with a smile. "What was I thinking, really? Of course we need to stay out of it. I—oh look," she cut herself off. "Enzo!" She called out the old man's name as she hurried toward him, Adam following closely. "I am so glad to see you. You look well."

Still surprised by the change in Elise's attitude toward the police investigation, Adam barely followed the few words the two exchanged in French. Enzo did look better, that was for sure. Despite a bruise still flowering on his right cheek and the cane the old man leaned heavily on, it was clear he was healing. His attitude was as grumpy as ever, which Adam took as a good sign.

"Enzo says he is fine," Elise explained for Adam's benefit as Enzo grunted out a sound of agreement.

"Stop fussing," he muttered, though Adam thought he detected a hint of appreciation for Elise's obvious concern. "I am simply shopping, that is all. No reason to be so excited."

"We're just glad you're feeling better, Enzo," Adam explained. "No fussing intended."

The old man grunted again and looked like he was about to complain about something else, when a shadow crossed his face and his eyes widened. Adam followed his stare. Sebastien had appeared at the end of the row of stalls, and if his clenched fists and scowling expression were anything to go by, he was not in a good mood.

Enzo's shopping bag clattered to the ground, paper wrapped packages tumbling onto the pavement.

"Oh, Enzo, let me help." Elise bent to retrieve his purchases and re-stuff them into his shopping bag.

Adam kept his attention on Enzo as the old man steadfastly looked away from Sebastien. Once he had his shopping in hand again, he offered the two no more than a brief wave and hobbled away.

"He must still be in pain," Elise said softly, shaking her head. "He shouldn't push himself."

"That wasn't pain," Adam replied under this breath, gesturing with his head to where Sebastien had stopped to glare at everyone around him. "That was fear."

"What?" Elise turned to watch the scene unfolding at the end of the aisle. "You think he's afraid of Sebastien?"

Adam nodded grimly. "And I'm pretty sure I know why."

"Sebastien!" Andrew appeared from the far street corner and jogged over to the other young man, draping an arm over his shoulder. "Thank God, you are out. They let you go, eh?"

Andrew was trying for a lighthearted tone, his words so simple that even Adam could follow them, but Sebastien simply glared at him in response. "*Oui*, I am out. No thanks to my so-called friends."

Movement on the far corner caught Adam's eye and he turned to see Chief Roche stepping back against a building. If he'd just finished a conversation with Andrew, he clearly didn't want to be part of the meeting with Sebastien. Julien looked toward Adam, who nodded a greeting. Julien's eyes then traveled to Enzo, who could still be seen retreating as fast as his cane would let him.

"Come, my friend," Andrew maintained his tone despite Sebastien's obvious anger. "Come, let us talk somewhere private."

Andrew led Sebastien between the vendors to a narrow street that led back toward Sebastien's garage.

Elise looked up at Adam, her eyes wide. "He is scary when he's angry, isn't he? Perhaps ..." she let her voice trail off.

"I agree." He nodded, guessing what she had been about to say. "I am one hundred percent sure he attacked Enzo. But Thomas ..." he frowned, chewing on his lip. "He's got an alibi that I just can't break. But if it wasn't Sebastien, then who?"

"No," Elise said, her voice firm. "You must drop this. I am sorry. I was crazy to think it would be good to be involved."

"You were worried about your brother, I understand that. But Elise ... you don't really think he was involved, do you?"

"Of course not, why would you ask that?"

Adam took a breath. "You seemed surprisingly concerned, that's all."

"No," Elise shook her head once, determination written on her features. "My brother is fine, and so am I. I was wrong to ask for your help. Please, let this go."

Something had gotten to Elise, but what?

He gestured for her to lead the way and they continued their casual perusal of the various stalls as they worked their way to the edge of the tarmac and back to the town square. Adam ran his mind frantically over everything he'd learned about Elise. About Andrew. About Sebastien and Thomas.

"Something's not right, Elise," Adam waited to speak until they were leaving the market. "I know it's not my business, but think about it. Sebastien has an alibi for the murder and a bloody weapon. Nicolas has a motive—"

"What? What motive?" Elise asked sharply.

"He inherits the winery, don't forget that."

"Pshaw, there's no money in that." Elise laughed at the suggestion. "Not yet, anyway, and not without Thomas."

"And I can't ignore the fact that your brother had access."

"Stop it!" She raised her voice and Adam spoke immediately to calm her down.

"But no motive. No motive, Elise. I can't imagine why he would kill Thomas."

"He wouldn't," Elise stated firmly as if closing the conversation. She glanced around, but no one had turned at her raised voice.

Adam spoke more softly. "There are a lot of people in town who hate Thomas' family, I'm learning."

"Of course, the Lefebvre family hurt many people," she whispered harshly as if stating something far too obvious.

"But that wasn't Thomas. Would someone really kill him to get revenge on his ancestors?"

"Aren't you here trying to find out about your ancestor? Isn't that important to you?"

"Touché." Elise had a point. He was hardly in a position to reject the idea that a tragedy from the last century could be motivation for a murder today. Even so, there were too many pieces to this puzzle and they just weren't fitting together. "There's more we could learn, Elise."

"Adam." Elise raised a hand, her brows furrowed. "No. I am telling you, we must stop. We are only hurting people. Uh-uh," she added as Adam opened his mouth to speak. "Do you still want my help on your own investigation?"

Adam nodded mutely.

"Then you must drop this investigation. Otherwise I will not help you."

Adam raised his hands in a gesture of acquiescence, then watched as Elise marched across the square back to her café and her home. He counted to ten. Took a deep breath. Anything he could do to calm himself, not let his anger take over. Because no matter what Elise said, he couldn't walk away that easily.

39

ADAM WALKED along the bank of the river, against the flow of the water. Leaves and small twigs floated past. Occasionally a tiny fish would splash. The water danced and sparkled in the late morning sunlight, glints of silver and bronze bouncing past on their way to another place, another world. Adam's eyes followed the water as he worked his thoughts around everything he'd learned in the past few hours.

Andrew had started working for Nico in the vineyard. Sebastien was back at work in the garage because Enzo wouldn't press charges. Adam couldn't understand that. Presumably Enzo agreed with Philippe that Sebastien was one of the good ones. They'd let him get away with anything. But even murder?

And what had he really found about his own ancestor, anyway? Yes, there was a French teacher who worked with someone to spirit Jewish children out of Poland. His instincts told him that was his great-grandfather, but he couldn't come this far just to accept a belief based on instinct. He needed facts.

He bent and picked up a long blade of grass from the river's edge. He stared at his hands as they folded it over and over again as he thought, the razor edge of the grass useless against the thick skin of his hands, the sharp scent of the broken blade lingering in the air.

Straightening, he saw the bent figure of a man moving slowly toward him. The man wobbled every so often despite his slow, careful steps, but he didn't use a cane or walking stick to support himself. Adam stood silently, watching his unhurried approach.

"*Bonjour,*" he said when the man was within hearing range.

He looked up, startled. His attention had been so focused on the ground in front of him, he hadn't noticed Adam standing there.

"*Bonjour,*" the man responded, stopped in his tracks.

"I apologize if I startled you ..." Adam spoke in French, but the old man furrowed his brow and shook his head.

"American?" he asked.

"Yes." Adam shook his head. Whenever he got too confident in his French, there was always someone there to put him back in his place, it seemed. "Yes, I am American. Good afternoon."

The man nodded and raised a hand in a type of salute. "I see you enjoy the river as much as I do."

Adam looked around them, taking in the sparkling water, the lush greenery and clear blue sky. "What's not to love?" he asked.

The man grunted an agreement. "And we should always be grateful for what we have, yes?"

Adam watched as the man took a few steps forward, continuing past where Adam stood, then took the somewhat forward move of joining him. "May I walk with you?" he asked.

The man shrugged, so Adam continued. "I am Adam Kaminski. I am visiting your town."

The man stopped again, his body rigid. He turned, his body moving first, followed by his head, as if he were reluctant to look back. Finally, he faced Adam and looked directly into his eyes. "Adam Kaminski," he repeated.

Adam nodded. "And you are?"

The man seemed not to have heard the question. His eyes ran over Adam, up and down. He frowned, sucking in his cheeks until his face looked like it would implode, his eyes narrowed to slits. Suddenly, to Adam's surprise, the old man's face broke into a wide grin, crooked and yellowed teeth exposed in a leathery wrinkled face. "I am very pleased to meet you, Adam Kaminski. I am Monsieur Kanoza."

"Oh yes, I met your son the other day. Or, uh, perhaps your grandson?" Even as he said it, Adam realized this man he spoke with now was even older than Adam had first suspected.

"Hm," Kanoza grunted as he turned his attention back to the path and continued his slow progress. "The youth, they tell me nothing."

Adam kept to himself his amusement at the idea of the middle aged man he'd met at lunch described as a youth. "It was enlightening, learning about the history of this town. About the war, and how you and your neighbors fought against the regime."

Kanoza raised an eyebrow. "We did not fight alone, you know. Tell me, Monsieur Kaminski, what brings you to *Saint-Honoré*?"

"I'm seeking information ... about my ancestor. Witold Kaminski. He was my great-grandfather."

"And you think he was here, in *Saint-Honoré*?" It was a simple question but the old man started shaking even as he asked it.

"No." Adam shook his head, hoping to calm the old man down. "I don't suppose he ever was."

Kanoza's shaking had stopped, but his face remained pale. "I must ..." he looked around as if lost. Or looking for something. "I must think. I must ..."

He turned away from Adam, his steps unsteady now. Adam wished the old man had carried a cane after all.

Adam knew he shouldn't chase after him, but he couldn't just let this go. "What do you mean? What do you know?" he called after Kanoza's retreating back. "You know about my great-grandfather?"

Kanoza didn't turn around but raised one hand. "Give me time. Give me time."

40

ELISE LET the earthy scents and silky smoothness of the fresh herbs draw her mind away from Adam Kaminski. She inhaled deeply, letting the smell guide her imagination, and she thought about how she might spice up the sausages she planned for her menu today. Nothing too drastic, of course, but she could always find new ways to combine traditional French ingredients into dishes that would both surprise and satisfy her regular customers.

Against her will, she found herself replaying that morning's scene in the market. It was good Andrew had been there to step in and calm Sebastien down, but what had he been talking with Julien about? Her worries about Andrew and what he might have done — or might know — fought their way back to the surface of her mind and she let the bunch of beets she was holding fall loosely into her vegetable basket.

Staring out the kitchen window onto the square below, she thought about her brother. He must be upset by Thomas' death. The man had been like a father to them both, taking care of them when they'd arrived. Not for nothing, it was true. He'd taken advantage of the opportunity to get Andrew to work for lower than expected wages. But she couldn't hold that against him. What businessman wouldn't want to save some money? And eventually it had paid off — they had applied for residency, got their work permits. And now they were both better off.

Andrew's work opportunities had fallen off, though, since Thomas' death. He'd been out early most days, looking for work in the vineyards that dominated this part of France. He had no vineyard experience, that was the problem. He'd worked the lavender farm for Thomas, but not the vineyard. Too many wine growers needed expert help, not just day laborers.

If only Andrew hadn't had to go off with Sebastien. She wanted to talk with him, ask him how his days had been, if he'd had any luck. Or any other ideas.

She had all of the food neatly stored and was wiping the last of the loose green leaves off the counter when she heard the front door of the apartment.

"Andrew?" she called out with relief. "Is that you?"

"Who else would it be?" he answered as he came into the kitchen. He went right to the fridge, opened the door and stared inside. "Anything to eat? I'm starving."

"Of course." She pushed him gently aside to pull out the dish of potatoes and cheese she had intended to be a side dish to their meal later. No worries, she could always make something else. "How's Sebastien?"

Andrew shrugged as he slid into a chair at the table. "I don't know. He's not happy, I can tell you that. And who can blame him?"

Elise turned to stir the cheese dish warming on the stove top to hide her face from Andrew, sure he'd see the guilt written all over it. "At least he's out now. And the police know he wasn't involved, right?"

When Andrew didn't respond right away, she turned back to him. "Right?"

He shrugged again. "Not involved? In what?" He stood, poured himself a glass of wine and returned to the table. "He didn't kill Thomas, if that's what you mean. They tried to pin it on him, but he didn't do it."

"Good." Elise brought over a plate of the warmed dish and sat across from him as he ate. "Good," she repeated. What did Andrew mean by that? Was Adam right? Had Sebastien really been involved in attacking Enzo?

"So talk to me," she changed the topic, raising the tone of her voice to sound more upbeat. "How's the job hunt going?"

"Great." A mouthful of food muffled his answer, but his eyes lit up. "I got a job."

"That's wonderful! Where?"

Andrew finished chewing and swallowed. "Right back on Thomas' farm."

Confused, Elise shook her head. "I don't understand."

"Nico hired me. Back into my old job. And," he paused for effect, his fork in the air, "he asked me to work on the vineyard as well. I'll finally get some experience that will help me branch out."

"Wow, that's ..." Elise struggled to find the right word. She finally finished lamely, "Wonderful."

"What?" Andrew asked with suspicion as he lowered his fork onto his empty plate. "You're happy about this, right? This is good news."

"Yes, of course it is," Elise responded briskly, carrying his empty plate to the sink. "It's just ... I don't know, isn't it kind of sad, to be carrying on like Thomas didn't die?"

"What are you talking about?" Andrew brought his glass over and put it in the sink next to the plate. He never seemed to question that Elise would wash his dishes.

She started the water and grabbed the sponge. "I'm sorry, forget it. It's great that you have your job back."

"And more. Don't forget."

"Why is Nico trusting you with the vineyard?"

"What, don't you think I can do it?" Andrew's good mood was quickly going south, but Elise had to ask.

"With Thomas dead, Nico is sure to be looking for someone to replace him — someone who understands wine, who can help him produce his first vintage."

Andrew shrugged and toyed with the apple he'd picked out of the fruit bowl. "I guess. But he already started — he showed me. He's got barrels aging in his cellar from this year's harvest."

Elise dropped the sponge onto the drying rack. "That doesn't make sense, I could've sworn ... anyway ..." She waved a hand at the thought, then gave Andrew a quick hug. "I am thrilled you have a job and you'll be learning new skills. I thought Nico said they hadn't started making their wine yet. I must have misunderstood."

"Thanks, Sis. I'm gonna go find Seb again, let him know about my job. Thanks for the snack." He called out the last bit even as he pulled the apartment door shut behind him.

From the sink, Elise saw him cross the square, heading toward the *tabac*. Why did Andrew getting involved with Nico worry her so much?

41

ADAM'S TIRES screeched as he turned too fast into the library parking lot. He'd made a beeline for Cavaillon after his encounter with Monsieur Kanoza. Adrenaline pumped through him and his hands shook as he thought about Kanoza's reaction. Despite his years of experience in reading other people, he didn't know what to make of the old man's emotional response to the name Kaminski. Combined with what Monsieur Bonnet had found, Adam didn't know if he should be excited or scared about what he could learn by pushing the old man harder. But he knew he would. He couldn't drop this now, when he was so close.

He also couldn't wait for Monsieur Kanoza to calm down enough to talk. He needed answers and that meant back to the library for more research.

He paused for a moment, his hands still on the steering wheel, looking up at the glass building through his windshield. His last visit here had been helpful, no doubt. And this time he had another name to research: Monsieur Louvois. The one person Adam knew had been involved with someone from Poland, involved in helping Jewish children escape the horrors of Nazi-occupied Europe. He just needed proof that the Pole working with Louvois had been his great-grandfather.

He kept turning over what he'd learned so far in his mind as he locked the car and walked around to the glass entrance on the far side of the building. As with his last visit, the library was well patronized. Adam slowed his steps to fall in behind a couple of teenagers on the path ahead of him. He knew a teacher in *Saint-Honoré* had been working with someone from Poland to save Jewish children. He knew his great grandfather had exchanged coded letters with that teacher. They must have been working together, he told himself. They must have been.

But he'd sat through enough criminal trials to know that all he had was circumstantial evidence. It made a strong case, definitely. But he still had that shadow of a doubt. He saw old Monsieur Kanoza's expression again in his mind when he heard Adam's name. Saw the man shake. Was that fear? Could he remember something horrible about Witold Kaminski?

A shout brought Adam's attention back to the present. He had just reached the front apron of the library, a wide, paved area beyond the metal fence that separated the street from the sidewalk. Here, long, shallow steps led from the street to the library. He turned to see who had shouted. He turned just in time.

A black Peugeot hatchback, which had been crawling down the road next to the library, sprang to life. As the car sped up, it swerved onto the sidewalk, causing the shouting from pedestrians. But it didn't slow. In fact, it sped up.

Dark tinted windows prevented Adam from seeing the driver, but he didn't need to make eye contact to know the car was heading right for him. He didn't think, he just ran toward the fencing. He heard more shouting as people dove out of the way of the careening vehicle but it was still pointing right at him. He could feel the heat of the car on the back of his legs as he took a leap over the first square of fence. Flimsy as it was, he needed to get something between him and the car.

The car swerved at the last second to avoid the fence but Adam heard the screech of metal on metal as a piece of the fence caught and dragged along the side of the car. Adam fell back against the wall of the library and watched as the car drove away. At least he would recognize the car if he ever saw it again, with that scratch along the side.

Unless the owner was someone who could get it fixed fast, without anyone else hearing about it. Someone like a mechanic.

People were picking themselves up from the sidewalk, dusting themselves off. A security guard ran out of the library and assisted those who needed help, guiding startled men and women to benches or to seats on the grass. Adam heard worry in their voices, though a couple of people were laughing. He knew it was just a nervous reaction.

No one else seemed to have noticed that the car had been targeting him. The guard checked to see if he was okay, but paid him no particular attention.

Adam considered his options as he took a few breaths to calm himself down. Had he imagined that the car was heading right for him? Perhaps that's what all accident victims felt in the moment. Or was he right, and something Adam had seen, said, or done had hit a nerve.

But what? Something he'd uncovered about Thomas? Or the information that Monsieur Kanoza was afraid to share?

If someone was trying to put him off, they chose the

wrong way to do it. He glanced at the library, considering abandoning this particular quest for now, but decided against it. Whoever had been driving that car wasn't going to get the satisfaction of driving Adam away — from the investigation of Thomas' death or his own research.

By the time Adam found the librarian who'd helped him the other day, he'd regained his composure. She was full of questions about the accident — he imagined it was the talk of the library today — but he had no further information to give her. Instead, he let her pull out more microfiche copies of newspapers that might contain information about Monsieur Louvois.

While she moved through the library gathering the boxes he needed, he took the opportunity to grab a cup of coffee in the small tea shop next to the study room. A beer would have hit the spot better, but sadly they didn't have any on offer. He ordered from the counter and took a few deep breaths, inhaling the comforting scent of ground coffee beans as he waited for his drink. Just as the barista handed his cup over, the librarian stuck her head around and waved to him.

Adam took the tiny cup and placed it carefully to one side, making sure it was back out of the way of other customers, and trotted over to her. Once she showed him where she had set up his materials, he hurried back out to the café to down his coffee before settling in for another round with the microfiche scanner.

As he approached the café counter, however, he stopped. His cup had moved. Not much, not far, but it was most definitely not in the place he'd left it. He glanced at the barista, but he was helping another customer. Adam sniffed at the coffee but picked up nothing beyond the familiar, earthy scent. He looked around the room and saw only a few other people, none looking his way. He nodded to himself, tossed the contents of the cup into the trash, and returned to the study room.

Maybe he was being paranoid, but someone had just come pretty damn close to killing him. And Thomas had been poisoned with something before he died. Sometimes paranoia was not a bad thing.

Adam tried to focus on his research, but his mind was spinning. Who knew he was coming back to the library? Who had he scared enough that they would try to kill him?

This was no use. He couldn't even remember what he'd just read. He abandoned his work and went to find the librarian to let her know he was giving up for the day. An elderly man shuffled up an aisle to his left and Adam started. He couldn't see the man's face, but surely that was Monsieur Bonnet. He jogged up the aisle to catch him, putting his hand out as he approached the man. The man turned, a smile crossing the stranger's face.

"I'm sorry, excuse me." Adam stumbled for words. "I thought you were someone else."

He lowered his head and tucked his hands into his pockets as he made his way back to the reference desk. Everywhere he looked he saw strangers staring at him. He was letting his mind run away with itself, seeing murderers in every aisle, every reading room. At least he didn't have to worry about seeing Sebastien, he laughed to himself. That young man wouldn't be caught dead in a library.

He turned a corner and narrowly avoided bumping into Sebastien. He caught his breath. The young man stepped back as Adam approached. Sebastien didn't smile, didn't nod, did nothing to acknowledge that the two had ever met. He simply turned away as if Adam wasn't even there.

Adam felt the heat rise to his face and knew he was

losing control of his anger. This was the last straw. Maybe the villagers of *Saint-Honoré* didn't want him around. Maybe they didn't want his help finding out what really happened to Thomas. But he needed to know the truth about his family's past, and if he couldn't dig it up at the library, then he would get it out of old Monsieur Kanoza. Whether he wanted to talk or not.

42

Business was slow this afternoon. Enzo huddled over a plate at a table in the middle of the café, while two women from another village shared a late meal along the far wall. They were all that remained of her lunch customers, and frankly, they were lingering later than she usually preferred.

Elise settled at her favorite table by the window and put Thomas' logbook in front of her. She thought she'd given Nico all the books they'd found for the winery when she'd asked for his help interpreting them. She hadn't realized that this book, marked for the lavender farm, also included Thomas' early notes from when he'd first started his vines.

Records for his investments in the vineyard were marked off from those for the lavender farm by two solid lines, nothing more. She let her eyes roam down the list of expenses: vine trimmers, electric secateurs, vats and presses.

Enzo coughed and Elise looked over quickly, but he seemed fine. As grumpy as he was, she was glad to see him back to his old routine, even if he was late finishing off his lunch before heading back to the *tabac* for his afternoon drinking session. He still sported a bruise under his right eye, but his gait had returned to its normal pace and his eyes held the customary glint of humor underneath the angry stare.

"Enzo," she said loudly so he could hear her. When he didn't respond, she said it again more sharply. "Enzo!"

"What?" he responded without looking at her.

"Tell me, what is a winery bell?"

He put his fork down and turned his head to stare at her. "A what? There is no such thing." He snickered and returned his attention to his plate, which Elise noticed was nearly empty. Why was he dawdling?

"It's written right here, I'm just going through—" she stopped herself before admitting to having the stolen logs. "I just saw it listed here among some winery equipment and I was wondering what it is."

Enzo didn't hide the suspicion in his eyes. "Winery equipment? Ahah!" He raised a finger. "A *cloche*. Ha! That is simply a nickname. For the metal hammer used to install vine posts." He chuckled as he picked up his glass and took a sip of water but didn't look away from her.

She shifted uncomfortably under his gaze, but returned her attention to the logs. Out of the corner of her eye, she saw him turn back to his plate and felt herself relax.

The door pushed open as Philippe entered the café, bringing with him the calls of schoolchildren passing in the street. He frowned and shut the door quickly. "Ah, Elise, I apologize for showing up at this hour, but is it too late for me to have some lunch?"

Elise bit back the urge to point out that it was well past lunch hour. "Of course, Monsieur Bonnet, please, have a seat." She led him to an open table and presented him with that day's printed menu. "We have only the Tartiflette left at this point. Is that acceptable?"

He agreed and Elise took his order back to Henri, who was almost finished cleaning the kitchen after the lunch service. He grumbled, but agreed to prepare the dish.

Elise returned to her review of Thomas' log. A few minutes later, she called to Enzo again. "I have another question, Enzo. Why would Thomas need waterproof light covers?"

Enzo put his fork down with a bang and turned to her. "What are you reading, Elise? Why can't you leave me in peace?" But she caught the interest in his expression even as he said it.

The two women sitting against the wall, who had been chatting away throughout her interactions with Enzo, looked over pointedly, as if her holding a discussion with a customer was somehow interfering with their gossip. They shifted their chairs so their backs were to her and Enzo. Philippe glanced over, but expressed no other interest.

Enzo stood and shuffled over to Elise' table, sinking into an empty chair. "Show me." He waved toward the log and Elise pushed it toward him.

"Here" she pointed at a mark in the log. "And here. That comes to ten thousand Euro. For equipment?"

"Well," Enzo shrugged, "he could have spent much more. But what does this mean?" The old man leaned close over the record to decipher a scribble in the margins.

"It says Nicolas." Elise explained. "I assume that must be Nico's investment."

Enzo chewed on his lips as he leaned back against his chair. "I thought Nico was only a small investor. This is half the original cost." He frowned as he thought this over.

"Well, then that is why he inherits the winery now. With Thomas' death, I mean."

"And the wine label," Enzo added.

"Right ... tell me, did you know Thomas had started making the wine? Nico made it sound like they hadn't."

"Oh, yes." Enzo showed enthusiasm for his favorite topic. "He consulted me each year. We both knew, immediately, almost before tasting the new wine, this was a good year."

"So now Nico gets all that."

"Hmm." Enzo slowly raised himself from the chair. "If he can keep it. He's no winemaker. Just an investor."

"A big investor though, right? Particularly for what he was getting out of it."

"What do you mean?" Enzo's voice was sharp.

"Look." Elise pointed to the third column. "The first year, at least, Nico was paid five percent of the profits from the sale of the grapes to a *négociant*. That doesn't sound like a deal Nico would make, does it?"

Of course, Elise thought to herself, now he owns the winery outright. And if Thomas really was already making the wine, already with bottles ready to be sold next year, that could potentially reflect significant profit in the years to come. If, and only if, he could keep the vineyard producing, and he could replicate Thomas' wine.

The café door flew open with a bang as Sebastien stormed in. Enzo, who had left a few bills on his table and was shuffling toward the door stopped short. He stepped back, as if to sit back down at his table.

Camille ran in after Sebastien and immediately spoke to Elise. "I'm so sorry, I told him to wait until Enzo was back in the *tabac*, but once he learned he was still here, Seb refused to wait."

"I don't have all afternoon, I have to get back to work," Sebastien said. "This won't take long."

Elise had jumped up when Sebastien entered, and now she stepped forward, between him and Enzo. She was relieved when she sensed Philippe Bonnet at her side. She didn't know how much of a defense she and the old man could offer against Sebastien, but at least she wasn't alone.

Sebastien frowned at her, then put both hands up in front of him and stepped back. "You misunderstand. I'm not here to start a fight."

"That's good, Sebastien. What can I do for you? Why are you looking for Enzo?"

Sebastien raised his voice and said, "I came to apologize to you, you stupid old man." He waved a hand toward Enzo, who leaned forward in his seat, listening.

"Go on."

Sebastien threw both hands in the air in frustration, pacing back and forth by the door. "I just did, you old fool. I regret that I ..." he glanced around the room, as if suddenly realizing there were other customers present. "I regret if I hurt you, that's all."

Enzo nodded silently. Elise laughed out loud. "Are you serious? You want to apologize? You must be crazy. That is hardly sufficient."

Sebastien shrugged, frowning. "I overreacted. He—" he pointed at Enzo "—was rude. Admit it."

Enzo grinned for a moment, then his face returned to a frown. "I admit nothing. Yes, you overreacted."

"So?"

"We understand you have a temper, Sebastien," Philippe said. "You've proved that often enough. You need to control yourself."

Sebastien's anger flared at the rebuke from Philippe. "This is not your business."

Camille stepped forward and put a hand on Sebastien's arm. He brushed it off, but she persisted, turning him to face her. "These are your neighbors, Seb. Your friends. It is everyone's business when you lose control. You know that. You're back at work now. It will all be fine, you'll see."

"You know Sebastien, Enzo. You know what he's like." Philippe leaned forward, his hand on the back of Enzo's chair, his face close to the other man's. "We know his people, yes? We must all accept who we are."

Elise watched the four of them, her amazement growing. Sebastien had violently attacked Enzo. He couldn't possibly be willing to accept a simple apology, could he?

Enzo nodded.

For a moment, the two men, one young, one old, simply stared at each other. Elise couldn't tell what was shared between them in that moment. Sebastien spun around and left the café, muttering to Camille that he was late for work and would see her later. She trotted after him.

"Enzo?" Elise asked, her voice loaded with questions.

"Pah." Enzo stood again and shuffled toward the door. "I know, but he's one of the good ones. All things considered."

43

It wasn't hard for Adam to find the Kanoza's address. A few questions at the grocery store got him pointed him in the right direction. Just a block and a half from the town square, the old house he found himself in front of now looked shabby, almost unlived in. He knew from his questioning that this had been the Kanoza family home for generations, but he also knew that only the older members of the family lived there now.

Two small windows let a limited amount of sun into the second level. Only one window joined the door on the ground level and its shutters were closed tightly. He balled both hands into fists, squeezing them tightly, and took a few deep breaths. He needed to get his anger under control. Kanoza knew something and Adam needed to find out what. Barging in on the old man in a state of anger would only scare him again, and that was the last thing Adam needed.

When he felt calmer, he knocked on the front door. Old Monsieur Kanoza opened the door, starting slightly when he saw Adam, then nodding and inviting him in. Only a few hours had passed since their conversation this morning, but Adam was hoping it was enough time. He needed to know what the old man had to say.

An inch or so of a yellow liquid covered the bottom of a glass perspiring onto the side table next to a comfortable chair. Kanoza has been enjoying a *pastis* when Adam had knocked. Something to calm his nerves, Adam assumed. But what did Kanoza have to be nervous about? What was Adam about to hear?

Kanoza grunted as he settled back into his chair, watching Adam, examining his features, his height, even looking down at his mud-covered shoes.

"I did not know your great-grandfather, Monsieur Kaminski," he finally said. He shifted his gaze to the blackened hearth to his right. Generations of his family had warmed themselves by this fire, the stones worn smooth and permanently gray from years of soot. "But I saw him. Oh, yes." He looked back to Adam. "Some of us will never forget him."

"Tell me," Adam realized he'd whispered the question, and coughed to clear his throat and ask it again.

"It was so many years ago, a different time, a different place."

"But here? In *Saint-Honoré*?" Adam asked.

"Here?" Kanoza frowned. "In *Saint-Honoré*, yes, in this house. But it was a different town then." He took a breath before continuing. "Monsieur Lavois, he was so brave. Even we who were young knew that. We wanted to be like him. To fight the way he did — not with weapons, but with knowledge. With friendships and connections. That is how one resists. That is how one wins the war. By undermining the enemy." Kanoza's voice had grown stronger, his hands gripped into tight fists on the armrests of his chair, and

Adam could imagine him as a young child, eager to stand up and fight the Nazis himself.

"What did he do?"

"He saved the children." Kanoza looked back at Adam. "I think you know this, yes?"

"I've heard about the kindertransport. I've heard that Monsieur Lavois was a teacher here in town who participated, who helped pass the children on, from Poland, through France to safety."

"Yes. And so was Monsieur Kaminski."

Adam inhaled sharply. "You know this?"

"Monsieur Lavois was killed. For his good work, he was tortured and shot." The old man's eyes clouded over and Adam felt a lump rising in his own throat.

"I heard that, too."

Kanoza nodded. "Once they had Lavois, no one on the chain was safe. Monsieur Kaminski had to escape, not just to save himself but to save his family as well." He looked back at Adam. "So that you could be here today."

Adam nodded but didn't speak.

"They had to get out, and they did — through France, same as the children."

"That's how you saw him?"

Kanoza nodded. "My parents, they wanted to help him. To thank him for all that he had done. He stayed one night in our house." He looked around again as he spoke and Adam tried to see the old, frayed furniture, threadbare carpets and chipped tile floor through his eyes. "I was not allowed to see him. My parents didn't want me to know any more than I did. But I couldn't resist, could I?"

He grinned, and once more the youth he had once been shone through. "I snuck downstairs, while the adults were

talking. I saw them, gathered here around the fire, whispering. He had your coloring."

Adam laughed out loud. "How can you remember that,
after all these years?"

"How could I remember?" Kanoza's eyes widened and
he furrowed his brow in confusion. "Monsieur Kaminski,
how could I forget?"

44

THE GROUP that gathered in the outdoor café was smaller today. It was late afternoon, just the time for a pre-dinner aperitif. Adam approached the square, knowing the group would be gathered for drinks, and paused, watching.

Years of life were gathered before him. Old men and women who knew each other so well their eyes shared untold words, younger people whose own lives had been guided by their elders and who looked up to them with respect and admiration. Wrinkles that gathered around eyes and mouths showed not only the trials and pains of years past but also the joy and hope of more recent times. A quick touch on a hand here, a whisper in an ear there, told Adam so much about these people. They were, indeed, a community within a community.

"*Bonjour.*" Adam approached the table. "May I join you?"

"*Bien sur!* Of course." Monsieur Kanoza the younger leaned back to pull a chair over from a neighboring table and settle it down next to his own. "Please, sit. What will you drink?" He raised a hand to flag the waiter.

Adam ordered a *pastis* and allowed himself a moment to enjoy the bittersweetness of the drink. And the company.

"I met your father earlier today," he said to his neighbor. "Walking by the river."

"Ah yes, he still walks. Every day, rain or shine." Monsieur Kanoza smiled proudly, but then the smile dropped. "After what happened to Enzo Marchand, though, I worry. He is an old man, and there is some kind of mad man in our town."

Others around the table nodded. "Enzo, Thomas, is no one safe here?"

Madame Gamay chimed in with a loud voice. "Do not worry, please. Your grandfather is strong. He has many years of life left in him, I have no doubt."

An elderly woman giggled at this. "He is like a boy these days, is he not?"

A few others around the table laughed, though Adam didn't get the joke.

When the laughter had settled, Monsieur Kanoza asked Adam. "Was he able to remember anything that was helpful for you?"

"He surely was." Adam felt himself grinning but didn't care. "He knew my great-grandfather."

"What?" Adam heard several sharp inhales around the table and knew he had won their attention.

"My great-grandfather, Witold Kaminski, worked with Monsieur Lavois. To save the children."

He glanced around the table as he spoke, knowing that as important as this history was to him, it was even more important to this group gathered here. Every eye was on him, peering at him as if peering into his mind, his heart.

"He remembered him?" Madame Gamay asked.

Adam nodded. "He only saw him once, but he said he

would never forget. And he knew that Monsieur Kaminski was Monsieur Lavois' contact in Poland. Helping children on the first step of their transport out."

A silent tear slipped down an aged cheek, another person coughed with emotion.

"Tell me, son," an old man asked him. "What happened to Monsieur Kaminski?"

Adam smiled again. "He got out. He made it to America with his wife and son. My grandfather." His words were greeted with nods, smiles and more tears. "They lived well, they had a big family."

Soft conversations sprung up in French around the table as members of the group turned to whisper to those sitting nearest them. Finally, one turned to Adam.

"But he never spoke of this? He never told his children what he had done?"

Adam shook his head. "He took that secret to his grave. I don't know why."

"I understand," Madame Gamay said, nodding. "It was vital to keep that secret. A matter of life and death. When you have kept something so important for so long, it is not easy to let it go."

Adam hadn't thought of that, but she had a point. After all the years he'd spent as a teacher, a police officer, and a friend to some fairly interesting characters, he'd never been required to act in such secrecy for so long. He couldn't imagine how he would react, but perhaps keeping that secret forever was the only way to let it go. To move beyond it.

He sipped his drink as the conversation around the table resumed its standard tone, though he was sure he heard the names Lavois and Kaminski pop up here and there.

Rays of late afternoon sun fell on his back, warming and comforting him, and he leaned back in his chair, stretching his legs in front of him under the table.

This was a beautiful town in a beautiful country. Filled with some beautiful women, he thought as he saw Elise passing by on the far side of the square.

No, he told himself, she was done with him. He'd found what he came to find, now he could leave Elise on her own, like she wanted. Pity, he could have seen them becoming good friends.

The gathering lasted only another twenty minutes or so, then the group slowly stood, with some grunting and cracking of knees. Adam kissed each person goodbye, more confident in his kisses now, then watched as they all made their various ways home.

When he was the only one left, he turned toward his hotel. Philippe Bonnet crossed the street in front of him, heading away from Elise's café, and he called out a greeting.

Filled with the peace of his recent encounter, he shared his news with Phillipe, suspecting correctly the other man would be as pleased as he was.

"Ah, how good that is for the descendants of the children. I am so pleased they have this new information."

"Do you know them all well?" Adam asked.

Philippe blew out his lips. "Well, it is a small town, is it not?"

"And you all have much in common, I suppose?" Adam asked with a lift of one eyebrow.

Philippe laughed. "We do not all live in the past, if that is what you mean, young man. Do not assume. But ..." he wagged his head from side to side. "I believe you share my belief more than some others that we must understand the past. It is never really behind us, is it, but rather always present."

"I guess I'm still a historian after all," Adam agreed. "Thank you, again, for all of your help. I could not have found this out without you."

"It was my pleasure, Monsieur Kaminski. A true pleasure."

Approaching his hotel, Adam realized he was too worked up to return to his room alone. He switched directions and headed to the *tabac*.

Even with this good news, he still felt a sense of obligation to these people, to this town. His great-grandfather had helped them, of course, but so many more had been killed. They were grateful to his family, he knew, but he shared that gratitude for them. For helping him find the truth and for not blaming him for the many who did not survive.

There must be something he could do for them. He couldn't bring anyone back to life, even if he could help restore some memories. But he didn't have the kind of money he would need to endow a museum or even install a monument. Plus, Monsieur Bonnet was a better historian than he'd ever been, so he'd leave the writing of history to the experts.

He was an expert now at something else. The only thing he could offer them: his skill as a detective. If the attack at the library told him anything, it was that he was asking the right questions and making someone nervous. He would solve this murder and help them feel safe in their own town.

45

Adam wondered what his sister would think if she knew he was spending his time moving from café to *tabac*. The usual group of smokers gathered around the front door. Adam suspected some of them to be younger than the legal age to buy tobacco in France, but he let the thought drop. He wasn't a cop here. Even if he did intend to look into Thomas' murder.

He hated investigating crimes when he was so far from the support of the department. Particularly the support of his partner, Pete. He toyed with the idea of texting Pete about his current situation, but he knew what Pete would say. This wasn't his business, wasn't his case. And Captain Hillyard expected him back ASAP.

He glanced back toward the town square before stepping into the bar. It could be his business. He could see himself staying in a town like this. Clearly, whoever had tried to run him down at the library thought he was digging too deep, getting too close. Too bad he didn't have any evidence that he'd actually been attacked, evidence that might get him the help he needed from the department.

Leaning on the bar, he waited patiently for Nico, who was dealing with a cluster of farmers at the other end. Adam had been here long enough that he was recognizing faces, though he didn't yet know everyone's name. He knew the tall man with the receding hairline managed the lavender farm across the river but liked to come over to *Saint-Honoré* occasionally to shoot the breeze with his competitors in the business. He knew the stocky older man, verging on fat, ran the garage where Sebastien worked, and liked to meet up with the farmers every so often. They were his best customers, Adam was sure.

Once he got Nico's attention, he ordered his beer then turned to lean back against the bar, watching the other men. Were they worried about Thomas' death? Residents of all the nearby villages must by now know he was murdered. The *gendarmes* had made their way to everyone who knew Thomas or had worked with him, asking their questions.

Adam had no insight into what they had found, but he had heard the grumbling from the villagers. The complaints that the *gendarmes* were poking their noses into people's private affairs. That they were pushy and loud. And even some grumbles that perhaps the *gendarmes* should be looking closer to home. To the people who knew Thomas the best.

Adam hated to hear that, knowing how upset it would make Elise.

The door to the *tabac* swung open once more, but this time the smoke that floated in brought a hush to the room. At the sudden silence, Adam glanced to the entrance. Two uniformed police officers stood there, looking around the space. A few feet shuffled, an old man coughed. Adam grinned. Sometimes it was fun being on the other side of this reaction.

"Gentlemen. Officers." Nico approached the two men, one arm extended. "What can I do for you?"

"Monsieur Morel, a moment of your time?" one officer said. The words would have been a question, but his tone made clear this was an order.

"Of course, of course." Nico guided them to a table in the back of the *tabac*, away from most of the other customers.

The customers all turned their backs to the three men, conversation slowly growing again, though Adam could tell it was more subdued than earlier.

Though the officers had spoken in French, Adam had been able to understand their request. It was hardly complicated. Encouraged by this small success, he took a few steps to his left, moving closer to the table where the officers questioned Nico. He picked up their voices, and focused on following their conversation.

One officer spoke in a low rumble Adam had trouble picking up over the other conversations in the bar, but the younger man's voice was slightly higher, carrying over the others. Nico's voice moved in and out as he raised and lowered it, clearly becoming agitated as he spoke.

"... from that area ..." the younger officer was saying, "... explanation ...witness."

Had Nico been in the area when Thomas was killed, Adam wondered? Perhaps he'd seen something without realizing its significance. Then again, even if he had realized it, Adam was pretty sure Nico wasn't the type of person who would go running to the police.

Nico was getting worked up, his hands moving as he spoke, his face getting red. Finally, he stood and pointed at Adam. "Him," he said in English. "He saw me, ask him."

Adam straightened, confused. "Saw you where?"

"Monsieur," the older officer spoke to Adam. "Did you see Monsieur Morel the morning of the murder?"

"Here, I was at work. I helped you," Nico said.

The younger officer put up a hand to silence him. "Please, Monsieur, let him speak."

"Yes," Adam said. "I saw him here. He did help me with some inquiries I was making."

The older officer frowned at Adam's mention of inquiries and seemed to be about to ask another question, but the younger man spoke first. "And what time was that, Monsieur?"

Adam shrugged. "I couldn't tell you. I'm really not sure. Oh, well ..." He thought for a moment. "I know I left here around eleven."

"But I was here all morning," Nico said to the officers. "He was here for some time, weren't you?"

Adam felt the eyes of all the other customers on him and knew the significance of what he was being asked. Could he provide Nico with an alibi? He thought back to that morning. To his frustrating conversation with the waitress in French. To Nico's grand entrance. To the waitress' comment that Nico was later than usual.

"No." He shook his head. "You came in late that morning. I remember. Ask the waitress." He glanced around the *tabac*, but she was nowhere to be seen. Adam realized she'd disappeared right about the same time the officers arrived. Interesting staff Nico had here.

"Adam." Nico's brow lowered. "You could not remember that so clearly."

"It was only a few days ago," Adam said. "I remember."

"Pah." Nico waved a dismissive hand. "He does not know. I will find Michelle, she will tell you. I was here." He looked around at his other customers, but they had all turned back to their drinks, none willing to make eye contact.

"You are bumbling about, looking for clues," Nico spat out at the officers, who sat silently and took his abuse. "You might as well ask Adam where he was earlier that morning!" Nico shot a dark look at Adam. "He was in Thomas' house, after all. Maybe that wasn't the first time, who knows?"

Adam stepped forward. Damn the man. Elise must have told him about their investigation.

"Oh, my regrets," Nico offered a blatantly fake apology. "Was that not public information?"

"Monsieur, perhaps you will come to the station with us? We must ask you a few more questions." The old officer stepped close to Adam ask he spoke. Again, not really a question. An order.

Adam sighed as he put his beer down. "Of course, Officer, lead the way."

46

"Your husband is a good man."

"I know," Margot replied to Adam with a laugh.

It was only thanks to Julien's intervention that Adam was heading home now, instead of still answering the *gendarmes'* pointed questions. In hearing of Adam's being brought in for questioning, Julien had taken the bold move of interjecting himself into the *gendarmes'* investigation.

He'd looked into everyone's actions that morning, he explained to the *gendarmes*. It was all in his notes. Julien had been able to confirm Adam's arrival on the morning of Thomas' death. He had checked in to his hotel, had a conversation with the owners, who had directed him to breakfast in the café in the town square. Others had seen him there, before he went to the *tabac*. There was no way he could have been out to Thomas' farm.

Of course, Adam had a harder time explaining to the *gendarmes* why he'd been in Thomas' house after the murder. He had become friends with Elise, he'd explained. She simply wanted to visit the house of a dead friend, to see if anything needed doing or taking care of. Now that no one was living there.

He explained all this to Margot as they walked. He'd met her as he was coming from the police station, she leaving the school. Both now walked toward the town square.

"I'm sure they still suspect you, then, of some involvement?" she asked.

Adam nodded. "I'm sure they do. I would, if I were in their place." There was no rule that said a murder had to be a solitary affair. It was perfectly reasonable to assume that even if Adam didn't kill Thomas himself, his actions in breaking into Thomas' house suggested guilt.

"I'm just glad they released you then," Margot said.

Adam took a deep breath. "This is all ... I don't know ... different."

"Different?"

"From what I'm used to, you know?"

Margot shook her head with a smile. "Actually, I don't know."

"Right," Adam laughed. "In my job, I don't know most of the people I come across during a murder investigation. Sure—" he held up a hand as she opened her mouth "—some of the snitches are regulars, yeah. And a lot of the bad guys are repeat offenders. But witnesses ... even suspects ... no. When I question a witness, I have no background information to go on. Just what I get from them. What I pick up from their demeanor, how they talk. You see?"

Margot considered. "But you do have access to people's background information. As a police officer, right?"

"Hmm," Adam indicated maybe with a wag of his hand. "We only look someone up once we think they're important to the investigation. Most people, it's not worth it."

Margot laughed under her breath. "I see what you mean, then. For Julien, he knows everyone."

"Hard to keep secrets in a town like this." Adam's words suggested agreement, but he knew differently. Not only had Julien not known who had been driving the black car in *Cavaillon*, he hadn't believed Adam's suggestion that he'd been targeted. He'd been kind enough to agree to place a call to the *Cavaillon* police, to touch base and offer the suggestion, but Adam had no expectation that the police in *Cavaillon* would take his fears any more seriously than Julien did.

He glanced over at Margot. These were not thoughts he needed to share with her now. Not after Julien had taken the extraordinary step of helping Adam that evening.

They walked a little further in companionable silence. Adam took in the gray and brown stone buildings, the back-drop of the hills still vaguely outlined in the dimming light, the sounds of parents calling children in for the night. It was idyllic.

"It is beautiful here," he said aloud. "So peaceful. I can see why people want to live here."

"People?" Margot asked with surprise. "No one wants to live here. The younger people are all moving out. To Avignon, Aix-en-Provence, even Paris. There is nothing for them in these small towns, they think."

Adam laughed in surprise. "I could live here."

"Could you?" Margot asked. "Seriously? As you said, it's not what you're used to."

Adam shrugged. They had reached the main square, where his path and Margot's diverged. They both stopped, standing looking out at the square. "Should I care about this murder?" he asked.

Margot gave him a questioning look.

"I mean," he explained, "I only started looking into it because Elise asked me, but now she doesn't seem to care. Then I thought I could help the town by helping the police, but they don't want my help. They suspect me of being involved. So who am I helping?"

Margot frowned. "Perhaps you are helping yourself?"

"Maybe. But why should I care, when no one else does?"

"Adam," Margot responded sharply. "Julien cares. I care. Many villagers care."

"Of course," Adam spoke apologetically. "I don't mean they don't care about catching the killer. I know they do. I just mean ... why do I care when I'm going back home anyway? Then again, what's waiting for me there?"

"Ahah," Margot let out a breath. "I do not know what waits for you at home, but you should know that moving here is not an escape, it's just a move."

"I'd escape from one set of problems but then only face another, is that what you're saying?"

"Absolutely. And of course, you must consider the many challenges involved in doing this." She paused, then looked over toward Elise's café. "But of course it can be done. Look at Elise and Andrew. They had a number of—" she stopped, cleared her throat "— let's say 'challenges' when they decided to stay. But they worked through it, sometimes around it. And now they're happy here."

"Elise told me about a few of her challenges. They had a bad experience back in Baltimore, I guess. Andrew was somehow involved in another murder. I know it scared her. I guess they came here to escape, didn't they?"

"Indeed they did," Margot nodded. "And our town is better for it." She looked up at Adam. "You should seriously consider this, Monsieur Kaminski. We can always use more good people in *Saint-Honoré*."

Saying goodnight, she continued down the small road that would take her back to her house. Empty, as Julien was still at the station. It would likely be a long night for him.

Adam was considering it. He might be happy here, who knows. He'd miss his sister, Julia. He'd miss his partner, Pete, and his parents. But would he miss the work? Was he ready to step back from bringing criminals to justice? Maybe it was time he let someone else take on that particular challenge.

With a nod to himself, he headed toward Elise's café. Even if he didn't stay here, just thinking about it proved that he needed to bring at least one more killer to justice. And though so many people in this town had hidden secrets, only one had blatantly lied to him.

47

ADAM FOUND Elise in the kitchen, doing some final clean-up and laying out what she could for the next day's work.

"Elise." Adam tapped on the back door of the kitchen, which stood open to the cool evening air.

She spun around at his voice, then returned to her work.

"Elise, I'm sorry that I was harsh earlier. In the market."

She put both hands on the counter in front of her and leaned heavily, her head hanging between her shoulders. He approached her, put a hand on her back. She stiffened at first, then relaxed.

Finally she straightened up and Adam could see that her eyes were red.

"I'm sorry, I am. I let myself get too involved in investigations. But it's the only way I know how to do them. I have to commit myself fully." He shrugged. "It's how I work."

Her face softened. "I understand, Adam. And I owe you an apology as well. You understand, don't you? I was afraid for Andrew. After his past experiences, I just didn't want him going through that again."

"That's why you first asked for help," Adam nodded. "I know."

"But now I realize that we really do need to leave this to the police. There is no role for you or me in this investigation."

"Hmmm." Adam glanced around the kitchen, avoiding her eyes. "No, I suppose you're right. But I can also tell you, based on years of experience, how valuable it is for an investigating officer when someone who knew the victim shares inside knowledge. It's the little things, things you might not think of as important, that can make or break a case."

"Like what?"

Adam shrugged. "Like … what his regular schedule was. Did Thomas go out in his fields every morning at that time?"

Elise nodded. "Everyone knew that."

"Ok, then … did he eat breakfast?"

"Coffee and a baguette. Like most of us."

"Was he ill recently? Suffering from headaches or dizziness, something that would cause him to lose his balance or fall off the tractor? Anyway," Adam held up a hand to forestall her before she answered as she shook her head. "I'm just throwing these out as the type of information that can be valuable to police, particularly police from another town who didn't know Thomas and don't know the villagers here in *Saint-Honoré*."

"But Julien knows us. And he's helping them."

"You heard what he said. He's not involved in the murder investigation. That's just the *gendarmes*. I'm only glad they made an exception tonight."

Elise looked confused. "But we've told the police everything we know."

"True." Adam pulled out a tall stool and perched on it. "I'm still going to keep my eyes and ears open, though. Anything I can do to help this town."

"Why is this town so important to you?" Elise asked with surprise.

Adam shrugged. "It's an amazing connection, I can't explain it. Knowing that there are people here who are alive because of my great-grandfather's bravery." He shrugged again. "I just feel like I want to protect this town and everyone in it."

"To preserve his legacy?"

Adam laughed. "Something like that."

"There is one other thing I haven't had a chance to talk to the police about." She filled Adam in on what she'd seen in the remaining logbook from Thomas' farm.

"Nico invested a lot of money, is what you're saying," Adam summed up. "And then agreed to a pretty bad deal for himself."

"Exactly. And ..." Elise dropped the towel she'd been holding into a tall hamper. "It makes me wonder where Thomas was going to get money from this year."

"What do you mean?"

"If he was planning to bottle the wine this year, that means he wouldn't be selling to the *négociant*. But the wine won't be ready for sale for another year. So he'd have one year with no income."

"He still had his lavender farm."

"True." Elise considered this. "True, that must have been his plan."

Adam watched her closely. "But you have doubts."

Elise shook her head. "It's just a thought. As you said, I'll share this with the police later. But for now," she looked around the room, "I need to find my *cassoulet* pan." She bent as she spoke, looking under and over shelves, moving pots from one spot to another. She suddenly stopped and threw up her hands. "Of course, it's in the attic!"

Adam followed her up the two flights of stairs to the entrance to her apartment. She reached up, grabbed a worn rope and pulled down a trap door in the ceiling. Stairs unfolded revealing a dark hole above them.

"Are you okay getting that down?" Adam asked.

Elise climbed the ladder, stopping with her head and shoulders in the hole. "I can see it but it's underneath another box." Her voice was muffled as she called down.

Adam tore his attention away from the shapeliness of her legs and stepped closer. "Here, let me go up there. I can grab them."

Elise stepped down and let Adam find his way up. "Watch where you step," she called out.

Adam stepped carefully, making sure the ground was secure under each foot before putting any weight on it. He knew how deceptive attic floors could be. He reached the pile Elise had indicated, the large, heavy pan below a stack of cardboard boxes. He moved one, then another, each time taking care to stack it safely. One box overflowed its folded flaps, a set of tongs sticking up between what looked like an old blender and an even older waffle maker. Clearly, whoever had packed this hadn't sorted things out before throwing them into boxes. He hefted a bag of old golf clubs onto his shoulder to get it out of the way then picked up the box.

Heading back toward the stairs, he called down to Elise, "When was the last time you cleared out some stuff up here?"

Elise laughed. "It's been a while. I think there are still boxes from when we first moved in."

Adam stepped toward the opening, still carrying the same load, the waffle maker sticking out the top of the box. "Things like this, you mean?"

Elise blanched, and for a moment Adam thought she would pass out. "Are you okay?" He set the box and golf clubs onto the floor and jumped down the ladder.

"No, no, I'm fine. Sorry. I haven't eaten enough today, I think. Did you get the *cassoulet* pan?"

"Right, sorry." Adam climbed back into the attic, grabbed the pan and carried it down to the kitchen.

"Are you sure you're okay? You seemed pretty pale up there."

"I'm fine. Listen, thank you for your help. I'm just going to have a quick sandwich before prepping the dinner menu. Do you mind?" She gestured toward the door.

"Oh. Right. Sorry, I know you've got a lot to do. But don't forget to go to the police."

Elise blanched again, her hand flying to her mouth.

"About the wine log?" Adam reminded her.

"Oh, right. Yes. Of course, I will. This evening."

"Tell you what, I'll take it." He held out a hand.

She hesitated, her eyes flicking nervously around the kitchen. "What? Why?"

"Let me take care of it," he said gently. "You don't need to be so worked up about this. I'll handle it."

She pointed to the shelf that ran along the back wall at shoulder height. Adam recognized the red binding and grabbed the book from the shelf.

"Thanks. See you tomorrow. And Elise," he looked at her carefully. "Take care of yourself, okay?"

She nodded mutely.

Adam walked out through the front of the café, wondering. Whatever had bothered Elise about seeing those boxes from the attic, it hadn't simply surprised her. Adam had recognized her expression immediately. That was fear.

48

ON HIS WAY to the station, where he was sure Julien would still be burning the midnight oil, Adam thought about Elise's reaction. What was she afraid of? And why was she reluctant to share what she'd found in Thomas' log with the police?

His thoughts shifted to the logbook he carried. Nico had agreed to a bad deal. He'd given money — a lot of money — for almost nothing. He already ran one business. He must have realized that at that rate of return, he would never make his money back. He didn't know Nico well, true, but that didn't sound like an action any good businessman would take. And if Elise was right and Thomas had come back to him for more ... his brows lowered and he picked up his pace towards the *Mairie*.

He found Julien alone in his office, the overhead lights off, only a cone of light from his desk lamp allowing him to read the papers strewn across his desk. It seemed like a mess, but presumably there was a method to his madness. Adam hoped.

He tapped on the door and Julien looked up. "Ah,

Adam. I was wondering who would visit at this time of night. Haven't you seen enough of this place for today?" he asked with a smile.

"Your friends not here anymore?" Adam asked in return.

Julien shrugged. "They took their conversation elsewhere. Back to their own headquarters, perhaps."

"Do they hold it against you that you jumped in when they were questioning me? I'm sorry if I got you in trouble."

"No, no, nothing like that." Julien waved away Adam's concerns. "Now, what brings you here?"

Adam sat in the chair facing Julien across the desk and laid the log down on top of the papers that already covered the surface. "This."

Julien raised one eyebrow and reached out a hand to flip through the pages. "This is a logbook for a business. Lavender and wine." He looked at Adam sharply. "Not only did you enter Thomas' house, but you stole property?"

Adam shook his head. "It wasn't like that, not really. We gave these books to Nico. It's his winery now, isn't it?"

"Adam, if I had known about this —" Julien cut himself off, his face turning red, his voice tense. He paused and pursed his lips before continuing. "I would not have defended you to the *gendarmes*. You must realize."

Adam took a breath. "I know, I'm sorry. But look, this is important. At least, it could be. Look here." Adam pointed to the entries Elise had highlighted for him.

"So Nico invested money in Thomas' business, so what?" Julien asked, the anger still plain in his voice.

"No. Look at the returns. Whatever Nico was, it wasn't an investor. At least not a willing one."

Julien's tone softened, his curiosity aroused. "Why do you say that? And why would Nico do that?"

"I'm not sure, but I can think of a number of dirty ways to convince people to give you money. Blackmail comes to mind."

Julien let out a whistle. "That is quite an accusation. It doesn't sound like Thomas. I knew him, not well, but I knew him. I would think ..." His voice trailed off, his eyes focused on something across the room. Then he shook his head sharply. "No, I don't believe Thomas would do such a thing."

"Are you sure?" Adam prodded him. "You just thought of something. What? Something Thomas did?"

"No, no, nothing like that." Julien waved a hand. "But there was ..." He rubbed the edges of a piece of paper between his fingers, his mind clearly going back over some memory.

"Think about it," Adam pressed. "Elise told me that Thomas hired Andrew when they first got here, but paid less than he should."

"Yes, well, that's true." Julien responded. "And Thomas' involvement in that crime — for it was a crime — is part of the reason we wanted to talk with Andrew early on about this murder. Of course," he looked pointedly at Adam, "I suppose you know, Andrew didn't have other options.

"Yes, I know," Adam said. "As far as Elise and Andrew are concerned, Thomas was kind to take him on. But Thomas was taking advantage of him, for his own benefit. You can't deny that."

Julien looked back down at the logbook. "I do not deny that. It was a criminal act."

"And how about all the times women in the village brought him food. Was he such a good friend that they wanted to help him out?"

Julien's expression was the only denial Adam needed.

"Then did they do it because they had to — because he had something on them?" An image of the photograph of a man and woman kissing came immediately to his mind. A man kissing someone else's wife.

Julien leaned back in his chair. It let out a series of creaks that made Adam nervous but Julien didn't seem to notice. He still held onto one of the files and as he thought he played with the edges until they were soft and creased. "You are suggesting that Thomas was an inveterate blackmailer." He spoke softly, adding, "and I didn't realize it."

"No way, I'm not holding you responsible for this," Adam said quickly. "Don't misunderstand me. But you know this town, you know the people. Is it possible? Or am I completely off base?"

Adam watched the emotions move across Julien's face as he thought about his village, his neighbors. He saw the fear, the anger, the embarrassment. Or maybe he was just reading into Julien's expression the emotions he knew he'd be feeling if confronted with a crime happening in his village that he had missed. Possibly missed for years.

Adam didn't blame Julien for not noticing the blackmail. If that was indeed what had happened. He knew how easy it was for small, unlawful acts to go unnoticed. Or perhaps noticed but ignored, too small to worry about. Except that they could add up.

Finally, Julien nodded. "Yes. It is possible." He raised an eyebrow and took a breath. "This is not a good thing, though, if it is true. If I didn't see it happening."

"You can't be everywhere, all the time."

"But if Thomas was blackmailing people that gives each of them a motive to kill him. Not just Nico," Julien pointed out.

"True," Adam agreed, chewing on his lip. "And another

thing I can't figure out is how Nico, let alone anyone else, could have hurt Thomas like that. Nico is big, sure, but Thomas was a big man, too. And he was on his tractor."

Julien snapped his fingers then dug through the piles on his desk to pull out a stapled sheaf of papers. "I can answer that. You'll remember," Julien grimaced, "I let slip that the medical report indicated traces of drugs in Thomas' blood. He'd been given ... what do you call it ... a 'rufy'."

"What? Here in *Saint-Honoré*?"

"Why not? GHB, this is what we found. Gamma-hydroxybutyric acid. It can be easily made. In a kitchen, for example."

Adam nodded, knowing it was true. "And slipped into something he ate or drank that morning. Elise said that Thomas always had a cup of coffee in the morning."

"Of course, who doesn't?"

"What if the killer put something in it? Just enough to make Thomas groggy."

"And make him an easy target."

Adam nodded slowly. "People don't change. A crook is always a crook. I think Thomas had something on Nico, and used that to convince him to 'invest' at a loss."

"I think Thomas had a way of convincing a lot of villagers to help him out," Julien added sadly. He shook his head. "I want you to be wrong, Adam. But what you're saying ... it rings true."

Adam sat back in his chair, encouraged for the first time since he heard about Thomas' death. He liked this, this back and forth. Working with a partner, sharing ideas, solving a mystery. He hated the politics of the Philadelphia Police Department. He hated the bureaucracy and the paperwork. But in the end, there was something about his job that he loved.

"So what might Thomas be blackmailing Nico about ..." Julien spoke like he was thinking out loud. "Nico has walked very close to the line at times, but I have never been able to prove it."

Adam raised one hand as if making a point. "For example, why are those teenagers hanging around outside his shop."

Julien stood. "I'll share this with the *gendarmes*. They'll want to talk to Nico. But Adam—" he paused as Adam stood, and held up the logbook "— they'll want to talk with you again as well."

———

ELISE FELT her hands shaking and tightened her grip on her shopping bag. She held her arm close to her body, the golf club pressing against her under her coat. Hopefully, it wouldn't be noticeable if anyone saw her. Though they could well wonder why she was going out of her way so late in the evening.

She wandered back and forth through the streets of the town, looking for an opportunity. She knew where there were trash bins available to her. At each location, she checked to see if there was anyone around. If she saw so much as a light in a nearby window, she moved on.

Finally, she saw her opportunity. The trash can behind the school was always available. It was shut away behind a wooden fence, but Elise knew from past experience that the gate was never locked.

She looked both ways, up and down the street, then eyed the building itself. All the windows were dark, no one working late, no students playing in the dark school yard. She stepped behind the school.

She moved quickly, trotting over to the fencing around the trash cans, pulling the gate open and sliding inside.

Once inside the fence, she pulled out the club. Maybe she should have wrapped it up? Or mixed it with other garbage?

No, she reminded herself, better to have nothing here that could connect her to the club. Just in case it was found.

And if it was found, so what? Someone might wonder why anyone had thrown away a perfectly good nine iron. But no one would ever think to connect it to a crime that happened such a long time ago, so far away.

49

Everything in the *tabac* this morning looked eerily familiar. The same rough-looking crowd standing at the bar. Two middle-aged men sat at a table sipping their sweet Vermouth, men who Adam now knew to be Eduoard and Jean-Baptiste. Luc, the well-dressed young man who managed the insurance brokerage, drank his coffee while reading the paper. And Enzo, strong, trustworthy Enzo, propped up the bar next to him.

Enzo grunted in greeting but said nothing more, turning back to his wine.

Nico was here promptly this morning, serving customers, restocking his cigarette and newspaper displays. He acknowledged Adam when he entered, nothing more. Still angry that Adam hadn't vouched for his alibi, no doubt. Soon enough, that would be the least of his worries.

Adam stood at the bar, his coffee cup empty, and looked around the space. He knew it well now. Felt comfortable, even. He could belong here. If he wanted to.

A movement to his right, from the back of the table area, caught his eye. Julien emerged through the door that led down to the bar's small kitchen. He caught Adam's eye and nodded. So it was true.

"Nico." Adam faced the man he called. "Tell me about Thomas. Tell me about the winery."

Nico, who was crouched down in front of his display cases, stood. "What are you asking? What do you want to know?" His words were calm but Adam saw his fists clench at his sides.

"I saw the logs, Nico. You gave Thomas a lot of money, for not a lot of return. Why would you do that?"

Nico's face reddened and he glanced around the bar. Not surprisingly, everyone had turned to look at them. Nico practically whispered, a harsh, grating whisper. "What you are suggesting, Monsieur Kaminski? Are you looking for a fight?"

"A fight? No." Adam straightened, standing tall but not moving toward Nico. "The truth, however, yes. I am looking for the truth."

"And what business is it of yours?"

"It is my business." Julien had approached quietly from the back room and now stood on Nico's far side, blocking the door. "I am asking, Nico. Tell me about the winery."

Nico glanced back and forth between the two men, his body tensed. Then he shrugged. When he spoke, his voice was normal. "What is there to tell? Thomas has ten acres on which he planted grape vines six years ago. Just to test it out. He had a feeling about the soil. He started with only a few acres, but wanted to plant more when he saw how they were growing."

"But to do that, he needed money," Julien prompted him.

Nico gave one curt nod. "That is true. He came to me. I gave him money."

"And in return?" Adam asked.

"In return, I got part of the profits."

"Not a very big part. You made a bad deal, Nico. Are you that bad of a business man?"

"Big? I suppose that depends on how you look at it. If the winery did very well, my profits would be big, as you say." He looked back at Julien. "Is this what you wanted to know?"

"And you agreed so easily?" Julien asked. "This seemed like a good deal to you?"

Nico did not respond.

"Thomas was ready to produce his own wine, wasn't he?" Adam asked. "In fact, he'd already started. I believe you have some of it in your *cave*."

"What of it?" Nico asked.

"That meant no sales to the *négociant*," Julien jumped in. "No profits this year. How could he survive?"

"We got the AOC label. It was a good decision. It would be profitable."

"Eventually," Julien encouraged Nico to continue. "But not immediately. How could he survive?"

Nico tensed once more, realizing they weren't going to drop this. His shoulders hunched as if standing against a strong wind, his hands in tight fists at his side, he bared his teeth toward Adam in the semblance of a smile. Adam wondered why he'd never realized before how wolf-like Nico looked. "You think I made a bad deal? You think I don't know what I'm doing?"

Adam shook his head. "Why don't you tell me? You were losing money, that much is clear. Did he come back to you for more?"

"I don't need to explain my decisions to you." He looked at Julien. "Either of you. This is not your concern."

"Then tell me this," Julien said. "Why do you have sodium hydroxide in your kitchen?"

Nico's stillness surprised Adam. He'd expected Nico to blow up. To yell, to show anger. Instead, he was silent. And perfectly still.

A cough from the table sounded loudly in the room. Adam took one step toward Nico. "Why did you do it?" he asked.

"Why?" Nico's low, growled answer carried into all corners of his bar. A word that carried years of anger. Of hatred. "Why?"

Julien took a step closer as well, but Nico turned on him.

"You did nothing. You are a fool. You have no idea what goes on in this town that you consider yours." He looked around the room. "All of you. You all know what Thomas did. Even you were getting closer to the truth, figuring it out." He glared at Adam before continuing. "We all know. Except you." He spat the last word toward Julien.

"Then tell me," Julien responded.

"I had no choice, did I? I had to pay him. Or you would have found proof that I was selling tobacco to minors." He glanced at Adam. "You look surprised. You think that is not worth blackmailing over?"

Adam shrugged, but Nico was right, he was surprised. Nico had killed one person and tried to kill him, for what?

"You know nothing. If I lost my license, what would I have? A *tabac* and *presse* but no bar? How could I make a living like that? Pah." His face twisted into a sneer, his eyes looking inward, seeing a memory, perhaps. "He said I should be grateful, I should be happy I was getting any return at all."

"And then he asked for more?" Adam asked.

Nico nodded. Once. "He came back for more. This year. To support him while he produced his wine. His wine!" Nico shouted. "As if I had nothing to do with it. As if I was nothing more than another tool in his collection. It was *my* wine! I paid for it. I owned it. And now I do own it."

Adam had questions, so many more questions. But he knew better than to ask. Nothing to lead Nico, nothing that Nico could later claim he'd only repeated because Adam had said it first. Julien, too, kept quiet. They both waited, hoping Nico would say more.

At that moment, a group of uniformed and armed *gendarmes* entered the bar. They must have heard enough. Four of them, but in their gear in this small place they took up the space of double that number of men.

"Nicolas Morel." One gendarme stepped forward.

"*Oui.*" Nico's voice shook and he moved back toward the wall.

"You are under arrest."

Julien, too, shook as he stepped close to Adam and let out a deep breath as the *gendarmes* escorted Nico out. "Thank you, my friend."

"It's always there, you know," Adam responded. "The anger. The seething hatred. It's the only thing that all killers have in common."

"You are far too familiar with this type of crime, I think."

Adam smiled slightly and nodded. "I guess so."

"It is not a healthy life you for, Monsieur Kaminski."

"No." Adam looked at the faces around him. The men were gathering their coats, bags, belongings, leaving this place that had been sullied with such actions and words, mumbling quietly among themselves. "Is this a healthy life, then?"

Julien grinned but didn't respond.

"And what of Nico?" Adam asked. "The evidence is pretty weak."

Julien shrugged. "Perhaps. But he will be convicted, I am sure. That was close enough to a confession, his words today. And we have the evidence that he was producing GHB. He must have given that to Thomas, to weaken him. The *gendarmes* heard it all. Of course, having a murder weapon would help, but in this case it appears the tractor was the murder weapon."

Adam nodded, picturing Nico approaching a groggy Thomas after he slid from his tractor. Grabbing him by the shoulders and slamming his head back against the tractor to make it look like he'd hit it in the fall. The *gendarmes* must have found some evidence of this on the tractor itself, some proof that Thomas couldn't have hurt himself in such a way by accident. Yes, having the weapon was often the difference between a conviction and a killer going free. Between loved ones finally having closure or never knowing who had struck down their brother, father or husband.

"You're right. Murder weapons can tell a story. Even after many years ... Julien, I have to go. There's someone I need to talk to."

50

ADAM PAUSED at the town square, once again admiring the peace and beauty of the place. He'd been here long enough, met enough of the villagers, to feel at home here, waving and nodding to acquaintances as they passed.

Thanks to his investigations, both for Elise and for his own purposes, he knew more about the townspeople than might otherwise be expected from such a short visit. He'd even dug up what he could about Elise and Andrew's past in Baltimore. He knew about the murder Andrew had been implicated in. Knew a man had been beaten to death outside a bar and that Andrew was one of only a handful of suspects. But no case had ever been brought.

He let his mind focus on what was really bothering him now. Nico had killed Thomas, that much he knew. He would face justice from the French authorities, one way or another. Adam knew he couldn't be sure that Nico would be convicted of murder, but he'd leave that up to the lawyers. His job as a cop was to identify the guilty party and get them off the street. It was up to the lawyers to follow through on the rest of the case.

He was packed and ready to go. He'd arranged for his plane ticket home, he just needed to jump on a train to Paris. All he had to do was say good-bye and walk away.

Which was why he felt so torn about what he'd seen last night on his way back to his hotel.

He'd been walking back from the *Mairie* and had just turned onto *Rue Nationale*, which housed the school. He'd caught a glimpse of someone ducking into the schoolyard. The furtiveness of the movement caught his attention more than anything else. The figure had been checking the area, and Adam could tell that the individual had just turned away or would have seen him turn the corner.

Intrigued, Adam had followed the figure silently, padding after it into the schoolyard, watching it duck behind some fencing in the corner of the yard. He waited in the shadows until the figure emerged. Until Elise emerged.

Catching his breath, he stepped back farther against the wall, sure the shadows hid his presence. She'd cast a wary eye up and down the street one more time on her way out, clearly not wanting to be seen.

He waited until she was far enough away not to hear anything, then followed in her footsteps to the trash cans hidden behind the fence.

With a feeling of dread, he lifted first one plastic lid, then another, until he saw what she had dumped. There could be no mistaking the golf club. He'd just seen it that afternoon in her attic.

So the question he had to deal with now was why was Elise trying to get rid of an old golf club? Late at night? With no one watching?

51

"I came to see you one more time before I leave," he was saying. Elise heard the words, but she also saw the questions in his eyes. The doubt. She'd seen that look often enough in other villagers to recognize it now. "I have to ask you, Elise." Adam paused, looking around the café. "I saw you last night."

She felt herself gasp. "Saw me?" Her voice was weak and she felt like a little girl. She forced herself to speak with more confidence. "What did you see?"

"Behind the school. Throwing out the golf club. One I saw in your attic."

She felt the blood rushing to her face, knew her own body was betraying her. "What did you do with it?"

He took her hands in his. "Tell me about it. What are you hiding?"

She'd spent a lifetime being the strong one, the wise one, the one who knew all the answers. She was tired, and she wanted someone to help her, someone to hold her. She wanted someone to help her bear the weight of the world.

She had no doubt that Adam was that man – she needed him to know the truth and to help her carry it.

She turned her face toward him and she told him, trusting him with their secret, with their lives.

She could still hear the bang of the front door that had started her out of her sleep late that night so long ago.

"Elise ... Elise, wake up." Andrew's whisper had a sharp edge to it as he shook her shoulders roughly.

She blinked and raised her head from where it had fallen onto her desk, papers sticking to the side of her face. She ran her hands through her hair and squinted at Andrew in the dim light. His eyes looked feverish in the glow of the small desk lamp that barely lit the room. His hands shook and Elise noticed they were covered in mud.

"What is it Andrew? What time is it?"

"It's 2 a.m. You need to get up, I need your help. I've really done it this time."

Elise stood slowly, working the kinks out of her neck and back. This was typical Andrew. Ever since they had been children, he had always just taken for granted that she would be there to watch out for him or help him out of whatever jam he had gotten himself into. But he wasn't wrong.

"Calm down and tell me what happened," she said through a yawn. She reached her arms up over her head, trying to force the blood to flow freely through her shoulders and arms again. "You know I'll help you, I always do." As she lowered her arms, she let one fall lightly onto her brother's shoulder and she smiled into his brown eyes.

"It's different this time Elise ... it's worse." Andrew shrugged her arm away and started pacing nervously around the room. Finally, he paused where he stood, with both hands on the mantle, and lowered his head onto his hands. When he spoke, she thought she had misheard him, his voice muffled through his clenched fists.

"What?" she asked quietly. "What ...?"

"He's dead," Andrew repeated. "I'm pretty sure he's dead." He looked up at her, tears in his eyes. "I didn't mean to kill him, I swear. We were fighting ... it was stupid, I don't even remember. We were at a bar, there was this girl, I was bragging about my new clubs." Andrew's words starting coming out faster. "He hit me first, so we took it outside. He was big, a big guy, and strong. I couldn't take him, I knew I couldn't. So I grabbed a nine iron – I had the bag in my car outside the bar."

He finally paused for breath. Elise stared at him with growing awareness. She could feel her adrenaline kicking in, making her arms and legs shake.

Andrew continued. "I hit him. I hit him. I didn't think it was that hard, just on the back of his neck. I just hit him once, and he went down. At first I thought it was cool, he was knocked out. I was actually disappointed there was no one around to see me take him out. But then he stayed down. And he was so still. So still." He hugged himself, finally sitting down on the blue sofa near the window. "He didn't move at all. So I walked over, and I saw the blood."

Elise realized there was no mud on Andrew's hands. She fled the room and ran to the kitchen. With trembling hands, she grabbed paper towels and ran them under the faucet. Staring at the water running down over the paper and her hands, she took a breath. She didn't need to think about this. Andrew had had problems with the police before. She knew how they would react. He didn't stand a chance.

She carried the damp paper towels back into the living room and sat down next to him on the couch. Gently, she wiped off his hands, first the left, then the right. Then she placed his hands in his lap and covered them with her own. "I will help you. I'll find someone who can help. We'll be okay, we just need to stick together."

Andrew nodded. He would do whatever she said. For as long as she could remember, she had always been the one who knew just what to do, how to fix problems and how to heal wounds.

The next day, she had given up her home, her friends, her life. She had cashed in her savings, sold what she could quickly, and used everything to help Andrew. So he could be free. So they could get away.

The past seemed so distant. Standing here in *Saint-Honoré,* she was talking about different people from a different world. But the crime she described was real and dirty, she knew as she was talking. Even the word – murder – felt like mud in her mouth.

She didn't know what terror she had brought to Adam's heart, but she saw the fear crease his face as she told her story.

In desperation, she kept talking, as if by not stopping she could prevent him from leaving. She asked him to help them keep their secret, to join them in their hidden world. He could retire from the life he knew, leave it behind, and stay with them. She knew he was considering it anyway.

He stood. Not roughly, but gently, helping her to her feet as he rose. He held her hands, and there were tears in his eyes. He nodded, but when he opened his mouth no words came out. She closed her eyes and the tears slipped down her face. He bent down, kissed her softly on her eyes, then left the house.

———

THAT HAD BEEN THIS MORNING. Now she stood waiting in her bedroom, staring at the window. It had become dark enough that she could no longer see the town beyond, only her own drawn face staring darkly back at her. Would he come to her, accept her for who she was, be willing to give up his old life for her?

With every sound from Andrew's room, every creak of the old house, she turned to look at the door to her room with expectation. Then she turned back to stare blindly out the window.

She heard the back door crash open, heard the heavy steps on the stairs. She jumped at the sound, backing even closer toward the window. They went for her brother first, he was the one they wanted, after all. He was the one who had committed the crime. He didn't know they were coming, she hadn't alerted him when she told Adam their secret. She had hoped, beyond hope, that Adam would come around, that he would come to her, hold her in his strong, warm arms, and offer the comfort she so sorely needed.

She had hoped for too much.

By then, they had secured her brother in the van in the street below. She could just make out its headlights in the narrow street. They were coming back for her, and she turned to face the door. Adam was there, with a group of men she did not know, men dressed in military gear, men with the *gendarmes*. He nodded at her, tried to meet her eyes, but she looked away, studying the uniforms and weapons of the large men standing in her room.

It crossed her mind briefly that this was too much just for her and Andrew, they hadn't needed to put so much effort into picking them up. That thought flitted briefly through her mind, but didn't settle. She focused instead on the only thing that mattered. She looked one last time at Adam, then lowered her eyes.

52

"YOU GOT IT, PARTNER." Adam ended his call with Pete, hung up the phone in Julien's office, then joined Julien and Margot who were waiting in the front room of the small police station. "Thanks for the privacy," he said. "Though you already know everything I told him."

Adam sat heavily on the bench and leaned his head back against the wall, closing his eyes and letting out a long sigh.

Margot perched next to him, placing a gentle hand on his arm. "I am sure your sister was happy to hear what you have learned here, was she not?"

Adam opened his eyes and looked at his friends. "Absolutely. My parents, too. I mean, they're not really as concerned about it as I am, but I'm sure they appreciate knowing the truth." He nodded as he rubbed his hands over his eyes. "God, it's been a long day."

Margot patted his arm one more time then leaned back on the bench. "You did the right thing, Adam. You know that."

He looked at her, and if her expression was any reflection of his, he must have looked stricken. He shut his eyes and shook his head without responding.

"Are you sure you want to return to Philadelphia now?" Julien asked, making the question sound lighthearted. "You seem to have settled in quite well to our way of life here."

"That is true," Margot added. "Though I don't think we need another police officer?" She raised an eyebrow to her husband who laughed.

"No, certainly not."

"So you're not in any trouble over the delay in reporting Thomas' murder and then getting involved in interviewing Nico?" Adam asked. "It seemed like your relationship with the *gendarmes* and *police judiciary* was on thin ice there for a while."

"Eh," Julien shrugged. "Perhaps. I think it will remain so. But the mayor is pleased with the results of the investigation. And with finding out how much Nico had been involved in outside the law — I stopped a blackmailer, made it harder for our teenagers to buy cigarettes, even prevented the village from being complicit in a fraudulent grant application." He raised both hands. "The mayor has nothing to complain about, does he?"

"An idea," Margot said as she stood up suddenly. She put a finger to her lips, then tiptoed into Julien's office.

Adam heard a drawer open and close, heard the clinking of glasses. A minute later, Margot reappeared carrying three glasses, a small pitcher of water and a bottle of clear liquor.

Julien laughed. "I thought I kept that secret better."

Margot rolled her eyes. "You cannot keep a secret from me, my dear." Margot poured two fingers of the *pastis* into the glasses, adding a touch of water to each.

Adam watched as the drink turned a lemon yellow as it

mixed with the water. It wasn't his favorite drink — he'd never been a huge fan of the flavor of black licorice — but he appreciated the gesture. And needed the drink.

"Add more water if you wish," Margot said as she handed it over.

Adam thanked her, took a sip, then added more water.

"I know I did the right thing," he said, finally responding to Margot's earlier comment. "I have no doubts about that. Andrew killed a man. Elise helped him cover it up. I had no choice."

Margot's face filled with pity. "I know you were becoming fond of her. We all saw that. I'm so sorry."

Adam barked out a laugh and took another drink. "Yeah, I have a pretty bad track record when it comes to choosing women. But at least this was the first accomplice to murder I fell for."

"I hope you don't let this stop you from meeting someone else," Margot said with a smile.

"Margot," Julien chided her. "That is not our business."

Adam laughed at his friends. "That's okay, I appreciate the thought. Hey, who knows what the future holds."

Though as he thought about his future, about returning to Philadelphia, dealing with the same bureaucracy, the same politics that frustrated him, he questioned the choice. Maybe he should stay here, in France.

"You really love this life, don't you?" he asked both Margot and Julien. "You have everything you need here."

Margot nodded and looked up at her husband, who offered a small shrug. "For us, it is right. But I do not think it would suit you, Adam. I get the sense that you need something more out of life."

Adam took a deep breath. "Good advice," he said. "But what?"

He finished his drink and stood to say goodbye to his friends, promising to stay in touch. He had managed to push his flight back to the States to early the next morning, so he wouldn't see them again before he left.

"Good luck, my friend," Julien said, grasping his hands. "I look forward to hearing from you, to hear what life has in store next for Detective Adam Kaminski."

AUTHOR'S NOTE

Wondering what was in Adam's psych eval? There's an easy way to find out! You can have a copy of the evaluation, which first showed up in *All That Glitters*, book 3 in the Adam Kaminski Mystery Series, mailed to you by signing up for my newsletter on my website, janegorman.com.

I hope you enjoyed reading *The Bitter Truth* as much as I enjoyed creating it. Of course, writing a book is never a solo effort. I am grateful for all the support I received from my early readers, mentors and friends who took the time to read, comment and critique, particularly Jennifer Meltzer, editor, and Bookfly Design.

I'd like to thank my friends and colleagues in the Sisters in Crime, both the Delaware Valley Chapter and the Guppy Chapter. Without your support, early reads, critiques, comments and creative ideas, this book would be half the story it is!

A big thank you to my France traveling companions, Dorothy and Kerry, who willingly tramped through endless towns and villages around the country to breathe the air, taste the food, experience the life with me.

Most of all, I want to thank Chuck, for his encouragement and unwavering belief in my writing.

In each of my books, I try to share the experience of traveling to a different place. I add touches of reality to give the setting depth and complexity. To make it more real. But rest assured this story is not real.

Many of the towns mentioned in this book are real, but *Saint-Honoré* is a figment of my imagination. The *Mediatheque* in Cavaillon is real, but the librarian, coffee shop and murderous driver are certainly not.

There are so many books I could recommend you read, if you're interested in what it might be like for someone to move to France, but I will limit myself to three (if you'd like more suggestions, just email me!). First, the witty, entertaining and oh-so-informative series of books written by Caro Feely, documenting her experience of moving to France and opening a vineyard. Second, a similar set of books by the actor and author Carol Drinkwater (though in her case, the books document the process of running an olive tree farm rather than a vineyard). There are so many great books out there in which wonderful writers document their experiences either living in or moving to France, you can easily spend years devouring them all. If you're looking for something more fictional (which I always enjoy), you can't go wrong with the Bruno, Chief of Police, series from Martin Walker.

Adam Kaminski lives on, in my mind and in the other books in this series. If you liked this book and want to read more, please visit my website to see the other books featuring Adam Kaminski as he steps up to the challenge of catching the killer, no matter where in the world he is.

To keep up on news about the Adam Kaminski books,

sign up for my newsletter or follow me on Twitter or Facebook.

Remember, if you're wondering what was in Adam's psych eval, reach out to me to have a pdf version of the psych eval emailed to you.

www.ingramcontent.com/pod-product-compliance
Lightning Source LLC
Chambersburg PA
CBHW030323200626
46816CB00006BA/1911